FINDING HAPPINESS

The Moondreams House
Romance Novels

Book Three

Ros Rendle

SAPERE
BOOKS

Also in the Moondreams House series:
Rhythms of the Heart
Lost and Found

FINDING
HAPPINESS

Published by Sapere Books.

24 Trafalgar Road, Ilkley, LS29 8HH,
United Kingdom

saperebooks.com

ISBN: 978-1-80055-907-3

CHAPTER 1

The bell tinged as Angela entered the gloomy post office-cum-shop. She made her way along the narrow little passageways between over-burdened shelves, finding the things she needed before waiting her turn to be served. Miss Brooks was serving a tall man. He half turned and nodded, then carried on speaking to the lady behind the counter.

Angela took in her crowded surroundings. The shelves were stuffed with everything from tinned beans to bottles of wine, envelopes, and packets of sweets. Then it impinged upon her consciousness that the man in front of her had an accent, possibly French. She looked at him with more interest. Her eldest daughter, Debs, was in France, gaining work experience with a vet, and she would soon be returning home to find a permanent job locally. Angela noted that the man's dark hair had a smattering of grey and touched the collar of his white shirt at the back. She couldn't help noticing that the shirt had come untucked a little but did not cover his neat backside. She was very aware of slim hips and broad shoulders.

Angela needed to move on with her life, but no, certainly not in that way. She chided herself and deliberately turned her head to study the shelves next to her. She hoped she had made the right move, coming back to this area. The familiarity was comforting, although she'd heard that Moondreams House had developed into quite a tourist attraction since she'd last lived here. She needed to recover.

As the man turned to leave, he nodded at her and grinned. There was a waft of something enticing that made Angela's heart thump as he squeezed past. His sleeves, rolled up, exposed very brown arms with dark hair that spread down to the back of his long-fingered hands in which he held his purchases. Angela dragged her eyes up to his face. He was at least a head taller than she, and she was tall and still slim for a woman in her mid-forties.

"*Madame*," he said, as he passed.

Angela nodded at him in confusion as she moved forwards.

Miss Brooks fixed her with a stabbing, unsmiling gaze. Her long nose and pointed chin echoed her sharp elbows and skinny frame. Angela waited while the lady's nails tapped the till. She didn't want the new neighbours to think her stand-offish, so she scouted around for something to say.

"My name's Angela Ross," she said. "I've just moved into Slater's Cottage with my younger daughter, Grace."

"Oh yes. It's been empty for a while. Old Mr Slater found things so difficult at the end." Her long face held little expression as she concentrated on her task.

"Old Mr Slater's daughter had a new kitchen fitted, though, so that's helped. It's just the garden. It needs a cultivator."

"Shame you didn't say when *Capitaine* Richard was here."

"Sorry?" Angela was puzzled.

"That man who just left." Miss Brooks nodded at the door. "You should go and see him. He's the gardener at Moondreams House and lives with his grandson in the Gatekeeper's Cottage. That's down at the entrance to the great house."

When she'd lived here as a child, Moondreams House had been run down and sad-looking, owned by a widower who shouted at curious children. Now, there was a little teashop called Tea and Sweet Dreams, and eMotion School of Dance used the old ballroom. Apparently the owner was now trying to promote the whole complex as a place to visit and was developing the grounds, so some things had certainly changed. Presumably, the French man was playing a role in that.

"French, he is, but a very nice gentleman." Miss Brook's sharp tones broke into her thoughts. "Shame about his grandson," she sighed. "Still, the lad would probably come and do it for you. Especially if you pay him." She leaned across the counter, lowering her voice to a conspiratorial whisper, although there was no one else in the shop. "I'm not one to gossip, but we all know. The lad's a bit of a tearaway. I think *Capitaine* Richard is pleased to have him properly occupied, if you know what I mean." She nodded and pursed her lips as she stood erect again.

"Thank you. Thank you very much." Angela packed her purchases into her cloth bag. "Gatekeeper's Cottage, at the entrance to the big house. *Capitaine* Richard."

"Right."

I'll have to watch what I say to Miss Brooks, she thought as she walked back home. *I'm sure anything I tell her would be around the whole of Waterthorpe village by sundown. Maybe tomorrow I'll pluck up the courage to go and find this Capitaine Richard. Depends how much of a tearaway his grandson is. I wonder why he has the boy with him. Maybe his parents couldn't cope.*

The writer in Angela sensed a story. It was the first prickle of true curiosity she'd felt since her husband's death.

Later that day, Angela took her dog Ranger for a walk in the quarry, which was now out of use. There was only a derelict station shed and an old wooden hut, and the land belonged to Moondreams House. Angela remembered that when she was very young, David Troughton, the owner of the whole estate, had got angry when children tried to sneak in here. Old Troutface, they used to call him, but it seemed he didn't mind the walkers at all these days.

Angela climbed over the stile and gingerly jumped down onto the rough grass. Her grey eyes skirted the field while she waited for the border collie to slither under the wooden fence. As she took in the scene, there was calm, and even joy, in her soul that surprised her. It had been a long time since she had experienced that.

A field of corn, still too green to harvest, was growing steadily. The poppies and marguerite daisies brightened the edges and she breathed in the scent of her childhood. She looked at the sky where this year's martins swooped to catch food for their hatchlings. The woodland, next to which she stood, was striped with sunlight, and the grass was filled with the humming of insects. Yes, there was still joy to be had.

As she turned, she surveyed the pockmarked land full of humps and dips from where the limestone for building Peterborough Cathedral had been taken nine centuries before. Ranger scurried and snuffled a few yards ahead as she set off again. The small hills were covered in closely cropped grass, but also scrubby bushes festooned with dog rose and creamy wild clematis. Golden cowslips and pink campion, horseshoe vetch and spikes of wild purple orchids were in abundance, and tiny blue and tortoiseshell butterflies fluttered everywhere.

As they turned a corner around one of the mounds, Angela stopped with a soft exclamation. No more than twenty metres away, cropping the turf, stood a magnificent fallow stag, its dappled coat glistening in the sun and its antlers standing proud. Amazingly, the creature did not see her or sense her presence. Then it must have caught the movement of her hand as she caught the dog's collar, because its head jerked up. For an entrancing instant, it gazed at Angela before it sprang away and vanished between the hummocks. She clambered up to the top of the next mound but, of course, the animal had fled. She sat on the warm grass and looked around, enchanted. Ranger scurried among the bushes, sniffing at rabbit holes and trailing scents.

Angela hugged her knees. It wasn't until she tasted the salt on her lips that she realised tears were streaming down her cheeks. Memories of her husband, Ade, had come flooding back. He'd died in a careless accident. She had begun to sense they were having problems, but the fact that she was here and he was not kept returning to stir her guilt.

Then a sound caused Angela to glance up, dashing away her tears. Her heart gave a violent jolt and she gasped, unsure whether to leap up or crouch lower.

Shambling towards her through the flowers was a man clad in a ragged duffle coat that was too large for him. It was fastened around the middle with strips of knotted polythene which Angela recognised as pieces of bread wrapping. Despite the sun, or maybe because of it, a hood, pulled well down, hid the top half of his face. His legs were encased in what looked like black dustbin liners bound crossways with reddish twine.

Angela took all this in as panic bloomed inside her. Notions of assault shot through her mind. Shocked into flight at last, she leapt to her feet and ran, shouting for Ranger as she slid and scrambled back to the path.

The dog came hurtling from some undergrowth and Angela clipped on his lead, casting a furtive glance over her shoulder before hurrying on towards the stile and the field. The man was making no attempt to follow but had in fact disappeared as completely as the stag, only minutes before. Nevertheless, she panted back along the path at the edge of the woods, glancing behind frequently and straining her ears for the sound of footsteps. The route that had charmed her now seemed full of menace. The trees hung low over the path along which she lumbered, and the stripes of sunshine within the thicket were those of a tiger hiding within. Every cracking twig, every bough shaking in the breeze spooked her as she ran, until her heart was beating hard. Reaching the stile, she scrambled over. Her lungs were tight and her leg muscles were quaking. Finally, a stitch in her side forced her to stop and lean over. She was still trembling as the roofs of the village came into view and the church spire rose above the hedges like an arrow to guide her home, for although she and Grace had only been at Slater's Cottage for two days, it was home.

Secure indoors at last, Angela filled a glass and took a long swig of cold water. Gradually her heart rate subsided as she sunk onto a kitchen chair.

I'll have to find somewhere else to walk with Ranger, she thought. She put her head in her hands. Just when she imagined things were going to get better, something came to smash her down.

Alone, the peace of the house began to soothe her. This ambiance was why she had finally chosen Salter's Cottage. It had embraced her with its peacefulness, and she couldn't resist when she realised she had to move.

Twenty-seven years ago, aged eighteen, when Angela had met Ade, she was still undefined, undeveloped, and vulnerable to the worldliness of the slightly older man. She'd married him, despite her mother's clear reservations and struggles to be supportive.

Ade had always been the strong one in their relationship. What did he get? Someone who spent years supporting him and his work, putting her own aspirations on hold. Someone who was excited and flattered to know she was important in this role. Angela was loyal, attentive, and encouraging, at first. Perhaps less so as the years progressed, and his expectation of her household prowess curdled into ungrateful acceptance. His ambition became grasping. She strove to find worthwhile activities. She became increasingly suffocated and frustrated with her lack of independence, but it had snuck up on her and before she knew it, it was too scary to break out. She adored the peace of the empty house after the children had left for school and Ade for work. The soft creaks, the muffled sounds of the street. Her isolation became a reward in which she revelled.

When the children came home like a whirlwind, raiding the food cupboard and fridge, they then usually disappeared into their bedrooms as teenagers do, and Angela smiled with her love for them and thought about preparing dinner. When Ade returned each evening, she pressed down the emotions that chafed her. Perhaps she sometimes wondered if he was as restless as she, but then she had to check whether they had enough bread for the packed lunches or that they all had clean shirts for the rest of the week.

Now, she would have to find greater strength from somewhere, to be self-reliant. Ade was gone. The release from acquiescence was daunting, but somehow, with the help of her sister and brother-in-law, Angela had managed to weave her way through the relentless rounds of solicitors and estate agents.

Then there were the worries about Grace, too. A new school at sixteen was not easy. It was early days, she supposed, trying to be positive. Hopefully she'd be all right when she got to know the place and a few of the other students.

Earlier that morning, Angela had stood at the window, watching her daughter walk up the village street to catch the school bus. Neat in her new navy skirt and blazer, the girl held herself very straight, shoulders squared, defying the world to see her nervousness, but Angela knew better. Her throat swelled with emotion. It was difficult enough for Grace to have lost her father so unexpectedly without being torn away from her school friends and all that was familiar, to be transplanted into this Cambridgeshire village among a host of strangers.

"The plain fact is, we can't afford to live in London anymore," Angela had explained before she put the apartment on the market.

"I do, like, get it Mum." Grace gave her a hug and never complained, even when the headteacher at this new school suggested she might attend for the last few weeks of the summer term to get to know the ropes and make some friends. If she passed her GCSE exams, already taken, she would move into the sixth form after the holidays.

Angela sighed. If only Debs could have been so understanding. She missed her father desperately, too, but it wasn't in her nature to be patient and calm about anything. Always so complicated, Ade and Debs had had an unspoken understanding that seemed to have evaded Angela.

Maybe she was too young when she'd had her. Debs had been a demanding baby — it had all been such hard work and Angela got nothing in return, not even a smile for weeks. She admitted it had been difficult to love her firstborn initially, so there were feelings of guilt on her part. Everything she'd read told of the mother and baby bond. Well, she hadn't felt it. Instead, she'd felt inadequate. If Ade hadn't insisted she go out in the evenings to that pottery course, she'd have gone mad. He was able to shut the door and ignore Debs's screams. Angela couldn't do that. Colic, the midwife said eventually. If she'd been told sooner, she might not have blamed herself quite so much. She loved her now, of course, but Debs could still be prickly.

Angela made an effort to straighten her back and exhaled with a gust. She was becoming more confident and self-sufficient, but there were many different things to worry about now, and no one to share it with.

CHAPTER 2

Grace's first day at school dragged. She was ill at ease, especially when the girls in her tutor group crowded round at break, asking personal questions.

"Where were you before?"

"Where are you living?"

"Have you any brothers or sisters?"

All easy enough to answer. "London, Waterthorpe, one sister but she's ten years older and a vet. She's working in France at the moment."

"Awesome, I bet she's clever."

"Mm. I suppose she is," Grace answered vaguely.

But when they asked the next question, there was an awkward moment. Silence dragged, until she said, "He was killed in a motorbike accident a few months ago."

All eyes avoided hers until one girl, Milly Paige, said, "I live in the next village, Millthorpe. I went to primary school in Waterthorpe. Saw you on the bus this morning, I think. I'll show you where the cafeteria is at lunchtime, shall I?" She gazed at Grace with large brown eyes, and Grace was absurdly grateful to her.

"By the way, sandals aren't, yer know, like, school uniform," a blonde girl called Tracey said with a sneer before turning back to her friends. "Better watch out. Teachers can get jammed over the smallest thing," she added over her shoulder. She had introduced herself as Tracey Sutton, also from Millthorpe.

The girls carried on chatting and Grace stood on the edge of the group, silently looking from one to the other and knowing she didn't belong. Her breathing became shallow, and her shoulders tensed.

How do I get away? Do I just wander off? Perhaps I better hang around. They might think I'm stuck-up or something. Oh, I so don't want to be here.

Her attention wandered to some older boys kicking a football about on an open grassed area. One, a thin lad with curly, dark hair, deliberately aimed it at the group of girls.

"You're a lousy shot, Q Richard," shouted Tracey. "Good job you're not in the England squad." She grabbed the ball and tossed it to one of her companions. Immediately, the girls spread out and began passing the ball from one to another. The boys, howling for vengeance, stormed up to try and recover it. When it came flying at Grace's head, she missed the catch. The boy, Q, pounced with triumph.

"Rubbish throw, Tracey," he shouted. Then he turned to Grace. "You're a feeb, new girl. Ducking instead of jumping and catching." Grace's eyes were stinging and hot, but she refused to let the tears come, so she sniffed and turned away instead.

He sent the ball hurtling across the grass with one hefty kick and several girls galloped in pursuit. The game became a general scrimmage. Left standing, Grace smarted. She'd failed her first test among the others and had been called a feeb by the hottest boy she'd ever seen. Q? She couldn't think of any name beginning with that. His grin had been mischievous, but he knew that, she could tell. Arrogant sod. Relying on his charm to get any girl he fancied just by smiling at her. Well, if he tried that with *her*, he'd be in for a disappointment. Feeb indeed.

Later, Milly took her to the cafeteria and then left her to fend for herself. Most of them had brought sandwiches, which they took outside in good weather to eat at some picnic tables under a shade sail. Grace determined to do the same another day. Their curiosity satisfied, they took no further notice of her and by the end of the afternoon, she was lonely and depressed, very much the outsider. School friendships had been long formed and although she had been shown some initial perfunctory kindness, it was evident that she was not to be easily included in any well-established cliques.

Grace anticipated the rush from the classroom at the end of the day and hung back. Hers was on the first floor but when she joined the crowd in the corridor, she was swept along the passage towards the stairhead. Halfway down someone's heel caught in her sandal, and the strap broke so that she stumbled and almost fell. As she stood waiting for the passing rush, shoulders jostled and vague swearing came at her. She took off her shoe and limped to the cloakroom, wondering where she might find some string or something to do a repair. A mêlée of girls, all pushing to get outside, rushed at Grace head-on. To find the bus for home, she hobbled outside with the offending shoe flapping uncomfortably, managing as best she could.

It hadn't occurred to her, and no one had said, that the school bus might leave from a different place from where they had been dropped off that morning. With dismay, she saw it vanishing down the drive. Now what? She knew the last public bus would have left for the villages much earlier and she couldn't possibly walk six or seven miles to Waterthorpe with only one shoe. She dug in her bag for her phone. Her Mum would come, even though she didn't want her to have to.

When she looked at the display, her phone battery was dead. How could she have been so careless? She'd have to find a public phone box. The telephone hadn't been connected yet at Slater's, but perhaps she could find the number from somewhere for Miss Burke or Brook or whatever her name was and ask that grumpy old bat at the shop to take a message to her mum. She had been strictly forbidden to hitch a ride and she was too scared to do that anyway. The school office would think her a feeb, too. She couldn't go there. This was all such a mess.

Grace understood why they'd had to move but ... oh, why did they have to move *here*? This place was a complete disaster.

As she stood outside the school gates, thinking she'd just have to grit her teeth and go back into the school office, a motorbike came roaring along the street and skidded to a halt in front of her.

"Hi, new girl. Missed the bus home?" The rider sat grinning at her. "That was a feeby thing to do, wasn't it?"

Grace pressed her lips together to stop her anger pouring out, but she eyed him coldly, determined to retain some dignity.

He glanced down at her feet. "Shouldn't be wearing sandals to school. Not uniform. You're lucky you didn't get done. Your first day, too. That's probably why you got away with it." He pointed at her broken one. "I saw you staggering across the playground. Well, hop on and we'll soon be home."

Surprise caused her to forget her disdain. "Do you live in Waterthorpe?"

"Yeah, with my grandad. Our house is the old stone one at the entrance to Moondreams House. *Grandpère* is the gardener there. I'm Q Richard." He gave his surname the French pronunciation with a silent 'd' at the end. "What's your name?"

"Grace Ross. We only arrived last week."

"I know. In Slater's, aren't you? Well, come on then. Can't stay here all night," he said carelessly.

Grace drew back, hot colour mounting up her neck. "Thanks a lot, but — no, I can't."

"Why on earth not? There aren't any more buses today, you know. Not planning to walk it, are you, with a broken shoe? Seven miles!"

"No." Grace's flush deepened. "Perhaps you could ask my mum to come across and get me."

He stared, then jeered, "Scared of riding pillion? You *are* a feeb."

"I'm not." Enraged, Grace decided to demolish him. "If you must know, I've ridden on the back of a motorbike loads of times, and one more powerful than that — my dad's Harley. But ... well, five months ago he was killed. Not his fault. Someone drove a van out of a side road without looking…" She stopped, overwhelmed by memory, her throat constricting.

Q Richard's face was almost ludicrous with shock. "Bloody hell. I'm so sorry. I'd absolutely no idea. Honestly."

He looked so genuinely distressed that Grace began to regret embarrassing him deliberately.

"It's all right. Well, I mean, I couldn't arrive at our front door on the back of a motorbike. It would really upset my mum. Anyway, I don't have a helmet," she ended lamely.

The boy's thin face was serious. "Look," he said, pulling off his own helmet, "you can wear my lid. I'll drop you off at the top of the village. We'll easily beat the school bus back, and your mother needn't know a thing about it."

"I will tell her." Grace wasn't going to have him thinking she'd lie to her mum, but she was still hesitant. "I can't wear your helmet. It's illegal to ride without one. What if the police stop you? It's dangerous, too."

He shrugged, a wicked glint back in his dark eyes. "I'll risk it. Had one ticket already — for speeding." He sounded quite proud of the fact. "Won't speed today, though, I promise." He grinned at her. "Unless you see the cops coming, that is — then you'd better keep your head down while I step on it, so they don't catch my number. Look, you can't get back to Waterthorpe any other way, except by walking, so don't waste my time. Hop on."

Grace did hop on. It seemed so much easier than asking her mum to come all the way to fetch her. Squashing down the guilt, she put on Q's helmet and they set off at a reasonable pace.

On the outskirts of the city, they passed the school bus lumbering north towards the villages. Grace wondered if she would be recognised despite the crash helmet. Her thick plait of black hair was likely to give her away. Hearing the other girls talking, she had gained a definite impression that Q's attentions were much sought after, especially by Tracey Sutton. She was unsure what her classmates' reactions would be if they realised Q was taking her home. She hoped that the bus driver would not report him for riding without a helmet. Q's curly head would be easily recognisable. He stopped before they reached the first Waterthorpe houses and Grace jumped down.

She returned his crash helmet and thanked him, but as she turned away, he said, "Why not ask your mum if you can get a skid lid? Then I'll run you to school every day. Save on bus fare." She turned back but he avoided her eyes and sat fiddling with the key in the ignition. When he did look up at her, he was smiling the same impudent, teasing smile but she was sure he had reddened a little.

"I'm pretty sure my mum wouldn't agree."

"Okay then, see you around."

He pulled on the helmet and roared off along the village street. Grace limped after him, meditating. She felt nervous about having to tell her mother about her method of transport home. She was anxious not to distress her but also determined that she shouldn't hear it casually from someone else. She bounced into the kitchen with artificial enthusiasm, where Angela was filling the kettle for tea, and had to fend off excited greetings from Ranger.

"Hello, Mum. Get down, boy, you'll make my skirt muddy."

"You're early, Grace. I didn't hear the bus go down the street."

Grace drew a breath. "Er, I didn't come on it. Missed it. It left from a different place from where it dropped us this morning, and no one told me."

"Then how…?"

"Don't be upset, Mum, *please*, but one of the sixth form boys brought me back on his motorbike." She saw her mother recoil and hurried on. "It was all right, honestly. He was really careful. I … I told him about Dad, and I'd broken my sandal strap." She held it up. "There aren't any public buses after two-thirty and my phone had run out of charge and our phone isn't connected yet and…"

"You could have gone to the school office and phoned the village shop," Angela interrupted in a tight voice. "I'm sure Miss Brooks would have brought me a message. I'd have come to fetch you."

Grace looked abashed. "I … I know. I suppose I could have, but I didn't want to bother you, and this boy, Q Richard, lives in Waterthorpe and…"

"Q?"

"Odd name, isn't it?" Grace gabbled. "His grandfather is the gardener or something down at the big house. They're French. Oh, Mum, don't look like that. He was ever so careful. Didn't go fast at all *and* he made me wear his crash helmet. I won't do it again. Promise. I just didn't know how else to get home."

"I don't want to restrict your life. I mustn't. I do know that. It's just … motorbikes."

"I know, Mum." Grace plunged forwards and gave her mum a clumsy hug. "I'm sorry and I won't do it again. Honestly, I won't."

"Did that boy suggest you could?"

"Well, yes, actually he did." Grace turned away and began fumbling in her school bag, so she didn't have to meet Angela's eyes. "He offered to take me regularly, to save school bus fares, if I got my own helmet, but I told him I couldn't." She looked up with apprehension. "I *did* tell him. I knew you wouldn't like it."

"You enjoyed the ride?"

"Well, yes," Grace admitted, aware of the heat in her face as she remembered her arms around the boy's waist when they rounded the bends. She hung her head again. "I was never nervous on the back of Dad's bike, and Q was seriously careful. You must think I'm awful."

"No, darling, I don't. I know how you've felt about Dad's accident."

Grace heard her take a deep breath.

"I told you, I'm not going to do it again, and I won't."

With that, Grace's throat closed, and she ran from the kitchen to the sanctuary of her bedroom before her tears fell.

CHAPTER 3

Gilles Richard sat outside his cottage with long legs stretched out and eyes closed. He listened to the sounds around him on the balmy evening air. A cricket, the water of the weir down the road, a blackbird. A half empty glass of lager sat on a small table next to him, and every once in a while, he tipped his head back and took a gulp. A smile tickled the corners of his mouth, and he breathed in deeply. Life could be good, and he was experiencing this more and more often these days.

The lilac and forsythia were long over, but two philadelphus shrubs were covered in sweet-smelling blossom. A tall buddleia by the gate was forming long cones of purple flowers for later in the summer, when doubtless it would justify its country name of 'butterfly bush'. This was not such a bad spot to have found after all that had happened. He drained his glass, sighed, and stood. He better think about food for the lad. He was so tall these days and always hungry. He needed to check whether he had homework, too, although he was loath to get into another argument on such a calm, peaceful evening. The last one had resulted in the lad dashing off on his motorbike and getting a speeding ticket. Then they'd had the most awful row. He'd banned the boy from riding it for a month, except then he'd had to ensure transport to school and back. He'd also had a sullen, bad-tempered youth under his feet.

Gilles was washing up in the kitchen when he heard the sharp tap of the iron door knocker.

"Q, will you get that? I've got wet hands."

He heard the thump of the boy's feet on the stairs and then a crash as he took the last three with his customary leap, then the front door opening. He stopped his task to listen.

"Is your grandfather at home? Could I speak to him, please?" A lady's voice, slightly husky but clear. It sounded quite sexy from where he was standing. He shook his head at his thoughts.

Then Q's voice called to him, "*Grandpère*, a lady wishes to see you."

Gilles heard footsteps on the stone flags of the hallway. He dried his hands with haste and smoothed them through his hair, before brushing imaginary specks from his denim shirt and grey trousers.

"Please come in," he said, trying to sound polite, as Q disappeared in a hurry.

He hoped she hadn't come to complain about his grandson giving her daughter a lift home. Oh yes, he'd heard all about that already, and not originally from Q.

He watched her looking around his living room. The old-fashioned range was spotless, the matte black paint grease-free. He saw her eyes wander over the blue and white willow-patterned plates that stood on the dresser; the old table that took up so much space, the wood scrubbed almost white. She bent to smell the crimson roses that stood in their pottery bowl near her end of it. Surely there was nothing here for her to pick holes in. The rag rug on the floor was rather worn, but he took it outside and shook it every other day.

"Please, sit." Gilles indicated one of the cushioned wooden-backed chairs either side of the empty fireplace and he took the other. He noted how she sat on the edge of it while he leaned back and tried to look relaxed.

"*Madame, bonsoir.* I believe we met in the shop?"

She looked at him like a startled rabbit, her eyes large and grey.

"You wish to speak with me? *Madame*, I am *Capitaine* Gilles Courtenay Qu'appelle Richard at your service. You must call me Gilles." He grinned at her to indicate that he was fully aware of the impression his name usually made and that it mocked him with its length and complexity.

He could tell she was flustered. Her hands were constantly moving, twisting her fingers and smoothing her skirt. She seemed breathless. Nevertheless, she was undoubtedly attractive with her slim figure encased in her blue flowered summer dress, with just a tiny glimpse of cleavage showing. Her short, dark hair was a little mussed from her walk in the evening breeze and she tucked it behind neat ears. She didn't wear a wedding ring, but he saw an indentation where one might have been.

"I'd better introduce myself," she said. "I'm Angela Ross."

"And you have a daughter with you, and another who now works in France to become a *vétérinaire*, yes?" Gilles remarked quietly.

"Well…"

He could hear the resentment in that one syllable and smiled. "Ah, *Madame*, please do not be angry that all the village discusses you. We are a close community and interested, but such curiosity means no harm."

"But this is not your original home, I take it. How long have you lived here, *Capitaine*?"

"Let me think. Q is seventeen. My wife and I and our daughter, who was Q's mother, came here from France when Q was five years old. We came here because my wife was English and lived here as a girl. This village is *village jumelé* —

er, a twin, you say — with my home town, St André de la Marche."

"Ah yes, that's where Debs, my older daughter, is — and that's also the reason she chose to go there, so not such a coincidence, I suppose. And your wife is not at home today?"

"She died two years ago, *Madame*. And Q's mother also, but before, when the boy was seven."

"Oh no, I had no idea." Angela became even more restless, and a frown creased her forehead.

"My wife, Marie, and I brought Q up, but now it's just him and I. We live together, the two of us."

"My husband … died a few months ago." Gilles saw Angela's eyes slide away and guessed at her clinging unhappiness.

"So I have heard. It is a sad, lonely time." Gilles ensured he spoke in a gentle voice. "But believe me when I say the sorrow will pass, even if the memories do not." He tried to inject some cheer into his voice and leaned forward slightly. "How may I help you, *Madame*?"

She explained her need of help in the garden.

"But certainly," he said at once. "I'm sure my grandson will be happy to do this work for you."

"The trouble is, the ground has become so hard and overgrown, it will need going over with a cultivator before digging. I believe you own one. Miss Brooks at the post office shop said." She shifted in her seat but still did not sit back. "Perhaps I might hire it?"

"I own one? No, no, *Madame*, I regret you have been misinformed. I have tried to persuade my boss, the owner of Moondreams House, to buy one, but he knows I can borrow one, so he prevaricates." He chuckled. "This is *Monsieur* Troughton for you. He has done much to improve the house and allows me to make improvements, too, but he is still careful, you know?"

She gave a polite smile. "Oh dear." She shot out of her chair. "I'm so sorry to have bothered you."

"There will be no problem." Gilles reached out to touch her arm gently with the tips of his fingers, calming her as he would a frightened animal. "It is Alan Cooper who lives at Home Farm on the corner of the road, just past here, who owns it. I'm certain he will be most pleased to lend it to us."

"Oh…" Angela appeared to relax marginally, smiling. "Perhaps I misunderstood. I may have had my mind elsewhere when Miss Brooks spoke. Do you think this Mr, er, Cooper might be willing…"

Gilles waved his hand. "Certainly, certainly. He has loaned it before for Q to use. You will permit me to walk with you now and make the arrangement? Alan is a good friend of mine."

"I don't want to put you to any trouble."

"It will be no trouble. We shall go, then?" Gilles crossed the room, shouted up to Q, and went to open the door.

As they walked side by side up the road, Angela said, "I must be clear. I insist on paying for using Mr Cooper's cultivator as well as for Q's time."

"That will not be necessary. Alan lends it frequently for Q to use in people's gardens. He never asks for payment."

"But…" she began.

Gilles looked down at her, saying gently, "Please do not worry."

Silence echoed between them.

"Q is an unusual name," Angela went on after a moment. "Have I pronounced it correctly?"

"Yes, like the letter in the alphabet. He is Bruno Courtenay Qu'appelle Richard, but prefers to be known as Q. It's how the

English friends he has grown up with say it. His full name, and mine, is an ancient way of styling in the part of France from which we come. Bruno who is called Richard. I am Gilles who is known as Richard."

"I see," Angela said. Gilles noticed a little frown of puzzlement flit across her forehead. With his habitual anxiety, he guessed she might be silently questioning why they had the same surname when he had already told her Q was his daughter's child, but she chose to say nothing more and he hoped the inherent question had passed. Perhaps she would think only of a child born out of wedlock. Not such a serious thing. Not like the whole truth of the matter.

CHAPTER 4

Angela was intrigued. The *Capitaine's* wife was English and local to Waterthorpe. She did not remember her from her own days here, but probably she was a little older and Angela's family had moved away when she and her sister were still in primary school. It did explain why the *Capitaine* had come here, but Richard had said his daughter was Q's mother. The lad would have had his father's surname, surely. Yet that was not the case. Perhaps he had been illegitimate and no father was on the scene for that reason. That might have caused some local talk in a rural French community, but it was scarcely enough reason to quit French soil permanently, surely. After all, half the kids at Grace's school probably didn't live with their original two parents.

They arrived at the farm entrance and her thoughts were interrupted.

"Alan lives on his own. He has built the farm up since it passed to him. It has been hard work for him. It was in a poor condition. He is a shy man but very genuine. I'm sure you will like him when you get to know him."

They entered through a little wrought iron gate that squeaked as Gilles pushed it. He stood back for Angela to go through, and then overtook her to follow the path. A yard was set to one side of the house, which was swept clean, and a stone barn with a corrugated tin roof reared up beyond that. She could see no further around the corner. Either side of the concrete path upon which they trod was scrubby grass but no flowers, and Angela was already thinking how it could be improved cheaply and easily. Bulbs under the window, perhaps a rose bed to one side would add colour but still make it easy to mow the lawn. Still, she had enough to do with her own garden and had drawn plans with which she was eager to get going as soon as the plot had been cultivated and dug. Angela looked up at the house. It needed redecorating. White paint peeled from the windows and sills and green from the front door.

The man who opened it after *Capitaine* Richard rang the bell was much younger than she was expecting, for some reason. Perhaps, like her, he was in his mid-forties. He was stocky in build with thick fairish hair, but he avoided eye contact. When they shook hands after Gilles introduced her, she was aware of rough, square palms that clasped hers strongly.

"Alan, *mon ami*, we have come on the usual errand. Mrs Ross wishes to make use of your cultivator. Q will do her garden at the weekend if that is all right."

Angela preferred to phrase the request herself and cut in. After all, she had come here to start a new life and gain some independence.

"*Capitaine* Richard means I should like to *hire* your cultivator, if convenient for you."

The farmer looked at her under his caterpillar brows before his gaze darted away to Gilles Richard, obviously embarrassed. It occurred to Angela that he was an intensely shy man, but before she could say more, Gilles Richard chipped in easily, "I have already explained that you are happy to lend your machine, Alan."

"Of course. You're welcome. When do you want it?" Cooper's tone was abrupt. He still avoided looking directly at Angela and had reddened under his tan. She decided it would be foolish to make an issue of the matter of payment.

"That's extremely kind of you." She made her voice brisk. "If we might have it on Friday evening, Q could make a start early on Saturday morning?" She gave Gilles a cool look. "I shall certainly *insist* on paying him for doing the work."

"But naturally, it is pocket money for the boy." He shrugged and although his tone was meek, his eyes were full of amusement, irritating her further.

She smiled tightly and nodded at Alan Cooper before turning to leave.

"I'll bring it round to Slater's on Friday evening, then?" the farmer mumbled. He suggested a time.

Angela turned, mildly startled. Her annoyance with *Capitaine* Richard had driven arrangements for delivering the cultivator from her mind, and she was even more embarrassed in case it was she who appeared rude.

"Thank you very much, Mr Cooper. That will be perfect. Good evening, *Capitaine*."

She marched off along the road, sensing their joint gaze on her back and feeling anything but confident. Gilles Richard did own the charm often attributed to his countrymen, she had to admit. But he was also too smooth.

I'm perfectly capable of making my own requests, she thought as she walked. *As for the other fellow…*

This caused her to slow her pace and take stock. Her natural generosity and sensitivity returned. It must be very difficult for a grown man to blush so easily and to be so ill at ease with others. She'd had to make herself go and knock on Gilles Richard's door earlier, but she'd managed it. That poor man, Alan, couldn't even look her in the eye.

Since she had completed her task and the evening was still mild, Angela decided to explore. She walked on down the street until she could cut across the field and then along the river and back to the main street of the village. As she passed an old mill, she looked again. Some of the windows were broken and others boarded up. The water of the race gushed under the huge wheel, but it remained still, and its paddles were covered in lichens and green slime. The river curved away in a wide arc to the right, controlled by a separate lock, but a number of boats were moored in a quiet arm of the water. She saw the Gatekeeper's Cottage across the way. Thank goodness she didn't need to go directly past it again just now, even though the French man might not be back there yet. There was a small iron bridge across the river and while she didn't want to go that far this evening, she went and stood in the middle for a moment to survey the scene. The water gurgled its way past the banks, sometimes with a small backwash as it descended over a steeper incline, and then seemed to rest in the shadows of the willows that washed their wispy fingers at its edge.

I've been cross and grouchy, she thought. *That won't do. But he got under my skin with his superior attitude.* Then her thoughts turned to herself. *Perhaps I was over-compensating in my nervousness and my need to be my own person. It has been a weakness to have been so reliant on Ade. Perhaps that's why he started to look elsewhere. All these years in his shadow when I thought I was supporting, I was allowing him to see me as his subordinate. Little wonder he got worse.*

Tears hovered again but she refused to let them flow, tossing her head and sniffing them back.

As she gazed into the darkness of the water below and took in the sound, it soothed her and she relaxed her shoulders.

What gives me the right to be so judgemental about these people? she thought. *But he is proud, this French man, there is no doubt of that. He manages on his own very well, it seems. Q might be considered a tearaway, according to Miss Brooks, but the boy was polite to me when he answered the door. He's been through difficult times, and it's a complex age for a boy growing into manhood.*

As she walked up the street towards her cottage, the postmistress was coming towards her. Speak of the devil. Angela was tempted to turn back or cross over. She wasn't in the right frame of mind to speak to this sharp old cocktail stick of a woman with her spikey tone. But it was too late — the lady stumped closer and lifted her hand in greeting, so Angela pasted on a smile.

"I've been to organise the cultivator," she said, determined to be friendly. "It doesn't belong to *Capitaine* Richard, though, but to Mr Cooper."

"That's what I said. I said Alan Cooper who lives near *Capitaine* Richard just on from the Gatekeeper's Cottage."

"I must have misheard," Angela murmured, knowing full well that the woman hadn't said any such thing.

"Poor old Jack Slater in that cottage where you live couldn't work in his garden for several seasons before he died, yet he refused all help," Miss Brooks was saying now. "A stubborn old fellow. He was ninety-two when he passed on."

"Older people do tend to prize their independence." Angela's thoughts returned unbidden to the strange man in the quarry who had startled her so badly. "I saw an old fellow in the quarry this morning. Like Mr Slater, I imagine, too proud to ask for help. I saw him when I was walking the dog. Gave me quite a fright."

There was a pause. It stretched out. Angela supposed Miss Brooks was considering. Then, at last, she answered.

"Old fellow? That would be Ben, I suppose." It was Miss Brooks's turn to evade her look now and Angela was aware of the immediate withdrawal in the lady's manner. "He must have been hanging around these parts for about twelve years or more, on and off. He's a man of the woods, a rough sleeper." The woman sniffed.

Sensing she must have given offence in some way, Angela hurried to make reparation. "A recluse, I suppose? How on earth does he manage to live, to get enough to eat?"

Miss Brooks pursed her lips, readjusting her glasses on the bridge of her nose. "How should I know?" Her tone was tart and bordered on rudeness. "He has his ways and means, I imagine. Got some hidey-hole up there in the forest, I expect. People have tried to help him." She looked sideways at Angela. "Folk do say he comes from a good family and is reasonably educated. I dare say he chooses to live like he does. Like an animal." She ended on an uncompromising note.

Angela had heard this kind of fable attributed to the dispossessed before; that he lived this way by choice. She was more than a little sceptical, but she murmured, "Really?" in a mildly interested tone. She knew, from helping out in the shelter in London before, that there were many reasons for homelessness — family rifts, substance abuse, mental health issues, redundancy. More often than not, rough sleepers suffered neglect and abuse from society, too, and often had insufficient resources to protect themselves.

"You needn't be scared of him, anyhow, Mrs Ross." Angela's attention was drawn back to the lady in front of her. "You can take your dog up there quite safely." The postmistress fixed her with a stony stare. "Ben's harmless. He won't bother you at all. You can take my word for that."

Angela made a few pleasantries and then managed to say her goodbyes. *Therein lies another story*, she thought as she reached Slater's Cottage.

CHAPTER 5

Grace stood at the bus stop with a small knot in her stomach. As the bus rattled up, she got on and looked around for a seat. Milly Paige and Tracey Sutton were already there, and Tracey indicated that Grace should take the seat immediately in front of them. Then she leaned forward and hissed, "That was you on the back of Q Richard's motorbike, wasn't it?"

"I missed the bus, so he offered me a lift."

"And gave you his crash helmet to wear. Lucky the police didn't catch you."

Grace turned and met the girl's angry green eyes with a cool look. "Q insisted I wore it. What's it to you, anyway? He simply gave me a lift."

"Well, you can't have him," Tracey snapped. "He's mine."

How blatant can you get? Grace said with disdain, "I don't want him, thanks. Anyway, I don't think he *belongs* to anyone." She turned to gaze out of the window as the bus lumbered past fields and scrubby hedges. She could hear the girls whispering but not what they said. She found her phone, plugged in her headphones, and found some music to shut out their insistent buzzing. Her cheeks burned. She wondered whether Q would speak to her at break but told herself she didn't care if he did or not. She found herself wondering with some dismay if he was indeed Tracey Sutton's boyfriend or whether it was merely wishful thinking on the obnoxious girl's part.

Grace saw him almost as soon as she left the bus. He was sitting on the low wall that divided the Sixth Form College buildings from the rest of the school. Tracey ran over to him at once and tried to muss his hair. He jerked his head away.

"Hi, Q. Saw you yesterday taking the new girl home." She tossed her head in Grace's direction, then tried to grab his arm. "Get off," he said, shaking her away. When he saw Grace, he raised his hand. "Hi." He jumped up and swung his legs over the wall before walking off, his school bag dangling nonchalantly. As Grace turned she saw Milly staring at her, brown eyes round and earnest.

"I think Q fancies you, Grace," Milly said as they walked toward the school entrance. Tracey stalked ahead.

"Oh, don't be daft. I told you, he only gave me a lift home because I missed the bus. I didn't realise it left from over the other side." Vaguely, she hoped that might be true. She didn't need to draw trouble on her head this soon.

"Tracey's nuts about him," Milly continued, "but he told Jack Hales that he can't stand her, I heard."

Perversely, Grace experienced an internal glow. "It's nothing to do with me. I hardly know him, or anybody for that matter."

There was an avidity about Milly's manner that made Grace uncomfortable.

"If Q falls for you, Tracey will scratch your eyes out." Milly said it with relish and giggled.

To get away from her, Grace went into one of the toilets. Leaning on the sink and hanging her head, she found she was pleased with the new information, despite her earlier thoughts. Then some others came in, banging the door open and making Grace jump. She turned on the tap and unnecessarily washed her hands.

She saw no more of Q for the rest of the day, and the girls ignored her during break and the lunch hour. They had presumably been friends since primary school, and she was the newcomer. They were probably just being thoughtless, but

Grace was lonely. She desperately tried to look as if she belonged and wandered about, looking for a quiet place to sit.

Q didn't come near her for the next two days either, and by Friday she was solitary, left out again and longing for school to finish. As she trailed out after the others to get the bus, Q appeared beside her.

"Hello. Sure you don't want a ride home on the bike?" His manner was a mixture of nonchalance and a supressed eagerness she could easily sense, and she became aware of a glow that spread up her neck.

"Thanks, but I mustn't. I told you why." She didn't mind showing her regret as she looked up at him sideways.

"Okay. I'll be up in the morning, then, to do your garden over. I gather your mum asked my grandfather to help sort out the cultivator."

"Yes."

"See you," he said and loped off towards the bike sheds.

Grace watched his retreating figure, the sun shining on his curly dark hair, and admired his tall, lithe frame.

Q Richard duly turned up on Saturday morning to cultivate the garden, but he was obliged to clear quite a few brambles first.

"I'll give you a hand with this part," Grace said, "but I need to find some secateurs and gloves first." She nodded at the old shed in the corner. "I hate it in there. It's all spiders and grimness."

"Show me, then," Q grinned and advanced towards the old wooden structure. "It's not that bad," he called over his shoulder. "Not being a feeb, are you?" He gave her a cheeky grin and this time she took his words in the spirit intended. "Where might they be, the gloves and stuff?"

She came up behind him and peered around his back as he bent to look for the necessary items.

"Maybe over on that shelf." She pointed past his right ear. She was still there when he reached forward, retrieved the things and turned to pass them to her.

Q nearly fell over her, not expecting her still to be so close. She staggered back. "Whoops, sorry."

Grace was aware of heat rising from her neck to her cheeks and her heart thumped. She bent to pick up a glove dropped in the flurry of the moment, and she was grateful to hide her face. She donned the thick gloves and spent the next hour and a half giving Q a hand. They gradually made a huge pile of clippings in the corner formed by the stone walls. At one point he teased her by waving a long strand of bramble at her with a big spider lurking among its leaves. She took it in good part.

"We can have a bonfire later," he said. "I know we've only just cut them, but they're old and half dead anyway."

"Next to no wind either, so should be fine. The smoke won't blow next door." Grace brushed a loose strand of hair away from her face and tucked it behind her ear.

"You've got a great smudge of muck on your cheek now." Q laughed, and pulling off his gloves he wiped his thumb across her face.

Grace was aware of her head ducking down into her shoulders like a tortoise, while heat engulfed her. She'd never had a boyfriend, not a proper one. This heart-thumping pleasure was a completely new experience.

When they went indoors for a glass of juice and some sandwiches, Q answered Angela's friendly questions with bashful politeness.

"No, I've really no idea what I want to do when I leave school. Mm, yeah, I'll have to do my A levels. *Grandpère* is so set on me going to university, but I'm not at all keen. I'd like to leave school right away, get a job, earn some funds and maybe get around the world a bit."

"You could do all that after," Angela said.

"Mu-um," Grace intervened.

"I supposed I can see some sense in getting qualifications, but the trouble is, I just don't have a clue what I want to do. Anyway, there are so many openings these days. Uni's not essential. Try telling *Grandpère* that, though." He rolled his eyes.

He reappeared on Sunday to finish the job and promised Angela he would come one evening to start digging. There was much laughter and calling across to each other with raised voices while Q operated the cultivator and Grace started the bonfire.

At the end of the day, they went indoors for a reviving drink, exhilarated from the fresh air, activity, and each other's company. While Angela's back was turned as she replaced a bottle of milk in the fridge, Q gave Grace a sparkling glance across the kitchen table and mouthed, "After school, Monday."

Grace was puzzled but had no chance to find out what he meant because he stood to leave.

On Monday, Q was nowhere to be seen. At lunchtime a rumour ran around that he was unwell so had stayed at home. The girls did not ostracise Grace, but neither did they draw her into their established groups, so after eating her lunch, she sat alone again in a corner and read a book on her phone, until it was time for afternoon classes.

By midweek, news had gone around the village that Q Richard had measles and was very poorly.

"Debs was immunised when she was six months old. It was a new vaccine back then, and you had it too," Angela said to

Grace. "Perhaps in France it wasn't automatic. Maybe I'd better call in at some point and see if there's anything I can do to help. Gilles Richard was kind in helping me organise the cultivator. I'm sure he can manage, still…"

In her new determination to be brave and independent, she decided it was the neighbourly thing to do.

CHAPTER 6

Angela and Grace's immediate neighbour was Pat Singleton, whose modern detached bungalow stood on the other side of the bridleway level with Slater's Cottage.

"Hello," Pat called over the wall to Angela, who was surveying her front garden in the morning sunshine and trying to see beyond the knot of rose bushes and weeds.

"Hello," she answered. "I was trying to formulate some plan for all this tangle. I've had the back cleared, but I thought I'd tackle this bit since it's not huge."

The lady introduced herself. Though some years senior to Angela, she showed every sign of wishing to be friendly. "I wondered if you'd like to come over for a coffee. I've just finished a mound of ironing and I've put the kettle on."

Angela learned that Pat's husband was a solicitor in a leading Peterborough firm. He travelled to the city each day in a grey Mercedes. The Singletons had two children, both grown up and married. She looked around the sitting room as she perched on the edge of the sofa. It was an expensively furnished room and was filled with photographs. There were couples at a wedding and some pictures of two pretty little girls and a bald-headed baby that Angela took to be a boy. Pat was evidently a doting granny who, eager to put Angela at her ease, told anecdotes about her family. Angela soon discovered that her neighbour was gently browbeaten by all the members of her family but thrived on it. A very different type of relationship to her own. This lady would never be an auxiliary to her husband and family.

"I'm so pleased you asked me here," Angela said. "Sometimes it's hard to be on my own after all these years."

"I can only guess."

"I've never worked other than in the home supporting my husband, so now…"

"Finding yourself again is always difficult and takes time, but you will." Somehow Pat Singleton instinctively knew what Angela was experiencing, and she was grateful.

As they sat chatting, the conversation eventually turned to the old man in the quarry and Angela described her encounter with him.

"Oh, yes, that would be Ben. So, you've seen him already?" Pat's cheerful expression clouded. "Poor fellow, it must be awful living in such a manner, but I suppose he's used to it. Once you're in that position, it must be virtually impossible to get back."

"I know: I saw plenty of homeless people in London. I read that there are thousands in this country and it's rising. There are night shelters for some, especially in the city, although many don't or can't use them. They're all so vulnerable. I used to volunteer in the kitchen at a shelter. But this guy, he did startle me the other day in that old quarry on the Moondreams House land."

"Ben's harmless," Pat assured her. "He's a bit odd, but he was probably a lot more afraid of you than you were of him. It's quite safe to walk your dog up there, anyway."

"Miss Brooks at the post office said something similar. She told me he's been hanging around there for several years."

"She did, did she?"

Angela was surprised by the sudden wariness in the older woman's eyes. It reminded her that the postmistress had seemed to resent her questions regarding Ben. Perhaps the village had some collective sense of guilt concerning the rough sleeper. "Miss Brooks said he's too proud to accept help."

"That may be so. Some people have tried, given him extra clothing and so on. I've heard he usually refuses such offers. Perhaps when you're in that state, as he is, all you have left is pride and independence. If you suspect there's an element of conscious charity…" Pat paused.

"It must be dreadful sometimes. In the cold weather, for instance — even worse if it's pouring with rain, everything getting wet and then staying damp," Angela said. "Miss Brooks was, well, almost rude to me when I asked her about him."

"Hm, Mary Brooks can be rather moody now and then," Pat murmured. She settled herself more comfortably in her chair, gazing at Angela with sparkling blue eyes. She had soft, snow-white curls and a pink face. Angela realised she was about to hear some village gossip.

"Of course, I've known Mary all my life," Pat explained. "She and I were at the village school together when we were little. Later, it was different. The Brooks family were well off, you know. Mary's father was a sort of unofficial squire around here, so Mary was sent to a posh school while we all went to the High School for Girls, those of us who passed the exam." There was no envy or malice in her tone, but her eyes twinkled. "Then Mr Brooks lost all his money during the oil crisis and recession in the early 1970s. Interest rates went crazy. Mary had to return from the finishing school on the French-Swiss border somewhere. Her father was very ill. I think he had a stroke or something and her mother had to nurse him. Mary had to get a job to keep them all. I mean, they had to sell the big house and everything. Mary was so resentful, and it's made her very bitter."

"It must have seemed hard, to lose all that."

Pat nodded. "Yes, but it's no use letting yourself get like that, is it? We all have setbacks. Some much greater than others, but often those people who are hit hardest are the ones who cope best. There are worse things than losing money and prestige."

Setbacks, yes, Angela thought. *Fear of deceit and of what might be happening behind my back. I should have tackled Ade about it immediately, when I had the chance. Now all I have are my suspicions, and guilt that I'm alive when he's not.*

Perhaps Pat noted something in Angela's expression, for she went on hurriedly. "We all want *you* to feel at home here quickly, my dear. In this village we reckon we're one big family. Cliché but true. Oh, of course, we do have our squabbles, sometimes real quarrels, like all families, but I've heard it said that Waterthorpe has a reputation for friendliness."

"Everyone has been really pleasant, greeting me in the street and being helpful." Angela's thoughts turned to Gilles Richard. He had been especially helpful. She pictured his broad shoulders, slim hips, and dark curls. Then his handsome face with the grin that made his eyes twinkle. He was just somewhat arrogant with it.

Pat leaned forward and looked earnest. "I'll be candid. I think it depends on *you*. If you're ready to join in, become part of the things we do, you'll be made very welcome. Some people have come and not done anything. Then they've gone again, pretty sharpish."

"I grew up in Waterthorpe. My father was the doctor. I can't see much point in living in a small community unless you want to be part of its life."

"How very sensible. Well, as I said, I've lived hereabouts all my life," said Pat, "so I know everyone. If I were you, I'd join the WI. That's a certain way of getting to know the neighbours."

Angela smiled self-consciously, wondering whether to admit that she expected to have little time for socialising, as she intended to make writing her full-time occupation. In addition, there were all the house and garden jobs she would now have to manage on her own.

Pat chuckled. "I'm president, for my sins, and I assure you we do try and plan a highly assorted programme. Why not come along and see? Judge for yourself. Second Thursday of each month, seven-thirty p.m. Then there's badminton on Tuesday evenings, and on alternate Wednesdays there's cards; lots of coach outings and a constant stream of coffee mornings and bring and buy sales for charities. Adult education classes, too. You can't stagnate in Waterthorpe."

Reassured by Pat, Angela decided it was safe to resume walking the dog in the quarry. It reinforced what Mary Brooks had said previously. Now *there* was an interesting woman. In the absence of anyone else with whom to talk about it, she and Grace decided her past misfortunes went some way to explaining her grouchy demeanour.

Ben was often at the quarry, and Angela retained a certain caution for a while, especially if she was on her own, which was the norm. It soon became apparent, however, that he was more nervous of her. If she came too near, or met him rounding one of the overgrown hummocks, he would scramble away amongst the bushes.

It was impossible to tell how much his way of life had aged him, but he possessed a straggly grey beard and glimpses of his face showed seamed and wrinkled skin.

Where had he come from? What had driven him into a life of such deprivation? Did he stay around here because it held some familiarity for him? Pat was probably correct in saying that someone in such straits would find it impossible to climb from that mire. No one would employ him in his filthy rags, even if he were capable of performing some tasks.

Angela recalled her time in the kitchen at the shelter. It was a half-hour journey on the train from Hampstead to Hackney, and although she sometimes wondered if she was just a middle-class do-gooder, she had worked hard and made some friends among the staff. Ade had thought her mad to persist with it. He often said she was playing at it to salve her conscience, but she thought she had genuinely helped one person, a man named Jeremy, who called himself Jez.

"This isn't my first time sleeping rough," he'd told her. "I've been on and off the streets since I left care at sixteen. My mum, she died in a house fire when I was six, and after that they just put me into the home.

"I started acting up after I was sent away. The school couldn't handle my behaviour and later my foster parents were always up there, but I was terrified of him, the so-called dad. He'd shove me around the house if I didn't do exactly what he said. I tried testing him all the time. I'd do something to irritate him just to see if this time it'd be different, but it never was. After that I was sent to a care home again, but that was even worse. There was always fighting, and I got bullied because I was weedy and small. I couldn't read or write properly either, so I played up in school or I just wouldn't go. I still couldn't read or write when I left care at sixteen. I couldn't even tell you the alphabet. I got into really stupid stuff after that. Stealing cars, shoplifting, drugs. I've done some bad things and I'm ashamed about it now. I got smashed in the face, pushed around. Scars everywhere. I don't want to be like that anymore. Looking back, I can see that I was just so angry when I was put into care. Twenty-two years later I've still not really dealt with those issues, but I'm starting to now. It started with a bail hostel, then prison. I learned to read and write in prison.

"I still get nightmares about the fire when my mum died, but now I'm trying to leave that life behind me and settle down. I met this girl. We'd like to get married."

Angela helped Jez get a job by scouring the papers and job centres. He started off as a cleaner at McDonald's. He wasn't too proud to do that sort of work. He had a genuine desire to sort himself out. Then, he got work in an office block. Eventually he became a caretaker with real responsibility. Last she'd heard, he had a child and seemed to be on the road to a settled life.

She doubted she could help Ben to that degree. Perhaps the locals wouldn't thank her for trying. They might think she was swanning into their territory and trying to take over. After all, she was the new one on the block.

CHAPTER 7

Later that week, Grace entered the kitchen before school. "I think I'll get my hair cut," she said, giving her mother a sideways glance.

"Good idea. It might stop you shedding hair all over the shower every morning. Wipe those crumbs this time, will you? You always leave such a mess."

Grace gave her a hurt look, put more bread in the toaster and turned away to pick up the dishcloth. They sat in gloomy silence, munching toast and marmalade.

Grace got up to leave. At the door, she said in muffled tones, "Do I have to go to school today? I could stay at home, pretend to be ill and keep you company."

"No chance. You'll never make new friends if you skive off."

Grace went and retrieved her blazer from the cupboard in the hall. The front door banged shut behind her and she trudged along the path, head down in the pouring rain.

Angela was filled with remorse. She was tired and irritable, having awoken with an overwhelming sense of guilt and loss, but she knew she shouldn't take it out on Grace.

Perhaps she should have done more to improve her relationship with Ade in those last few weeks. Did he have his accident because his mind was elsewhere? It hadn't even been his fault, but maybe his reactions were slower than usual.

If she hadn't decided to drive out to Kew that day, she would never have seen her husband with that red-haired siren, snuggled together. That's what it looked like. Her knees were trembling after. She'd pulled over at the first opportunity and taken deep breaths to steady herself. Over the next couple of days, she'd come up with any number of reasonable-sounding explanations, which in hindsight were pure rubbish and wishful thinking. This must be why things in the bedroom had been so intermittent. She'd reasoned it was because Ade was tired, overworked. Perhaps she hadn't been attentive enough, too busy organising that blasted presentation of her latest book and spending time at the shelter. She hadn't listened to him sufficiently, hadn't done this, hadn't done the other.

Her friends Jo and Harry always seemed to be laughing together; Sue and Elliot walked hand in hand. Angela thought it was charming, although Ade was dismissive of it. She still wanted to believe that they had shared special moments like her friends, even if they weren't in public.

Then her mind returned to that image of her husband and the red-head, and she was angry all over again — furious that he had died and left her with all these doubts before she'd had time to confront him.

It would have been so easy stay in bed drowning in depression, but she had vowed never to leave Grace to have a lonely breakfast on a school day. She had dragged herself up, donned her dressing gown and hauled herself downstairs.

Of late, she had been brusque too many times. She had wanted to say something affectionate before Grace left for school but was so consumed by the lethargy of her depression that she couldn't force herself to move. She stayed like that, long after hearing the front door bang. If only she could have shared her anxieties about Ade's behaviour before he'd died. There was no way she would do that with either of her daughters. She couldn't taint their memories of their father. As she rose from the table, Ranger watched with pleading brown eyes.

"You'll have to wait. It's pouring down out there." Angela stacked the plates in the dishwasher and went to get showered and dressed.

Her phone stared at her accusingly from the bedside cabinet. She picked it up and composed a message to Grace, apologising for her irritable behaviour.

Angela decided to go for a long walk before going to see Gilles Richard and Q, knowing that exercise was the best cure for what ailed her. The garden was too sticky with mud to do much out there. She knew she'd have to wait for Q to recover before it could be dug over and raked, ready for a new lawn and flower beds.

As she put on her walking boots, something shot through the letterbox. Inside the envelope, there was a card with a garish picture of a border collie.

Hi, isn't this ghastly? Debs had written. *Couldn't find a better one. Going to Jeannette's for a few days before I come home. See you soon. D.*

Typical of Debs to give no indication of when she might arrive, Angela thought with irritation. Jeannette Garot was the French girl who had been attending the same work placement as Debs.

Why, Angela wondered, did Debs always have to sound so … so terse? No word of affection. It was almost as if she despised showing emotion. She'd arrive eventually, clothes stuffed anyhow into an ancient holdall, hung about with plastic carrier bags filled with veterinary books and pamphlets. Debs's reading matter seldom included anything else. *She must think the stuff I write is extremely lightweight, if she's even read any of it*, thought Angela.

She clipped on the dog's lead and they set off for the quarry. A good walk would be the best way to get herself back on track. It had stopped raining, but the woodland trees still dripped and when they arrived the quarry floor was steaming gently in a sudden burst of July sunshine, making the air unpleasantly humid. The rough sleeper, Ben, was not in his customary corner. The ground would be too wet for sitting.

Angela let Ranger run free and was rounding one of the overgrown hillocks when she met Ben face to face. Before she could restrain the dog, Ranger leapt against the old man's chest, trying to lick his hellos. Taken completely by surprise, Ben sat back in a patch of thick, grey, chalky mud.

Horrified, Angela rushed forward. "I'm so, so sorry. Are you hurt? Ranger, come here!" She caught the dog and snapped the lead onto his collar. "Are you all right?" she asked the old man as he slipped and slithered and struggled to get up.

"It's all right, Missus. I'm not hurt. I'm not afraid of him, either." He pointed a gnarled finger at the dog.

His voice had the squeaky rasp of an unoiled door and Angela bent her head to catch what he said. She eyed the skirt of his ragged coat, which was slimy with mud.

"I'm so sorry," she repeated helplessly.

All at once, he smiled. Angela's astonishment was complete. It was a smile of quite extraordinary sweetness that illuminated his whole face.

"I'm all right," he whispered again huskily, and, now standing, he scuttled past her.

She watched him go, his feet squelching along the muddy pathway.

All the way home, she thought about him. The encounter had shaken her out of her introspection. The peculiar sweetness of Ben's smile stayed with her. Her curiosity, coupled with a new sense of compassion, intensified. She no longer had the least fear. She might be lonely and bereft, but she had a warm home, two daughters who cared about her, each in their own way, plenty to eat and decent clothing. The utter destitution of Ben's life appalled her as never before.

Reaching home, she stood in the scullery, staring at a pair of green wellingtons, nearly new, that had belonged to Ade. She had kept them when disposing of his other possessions, thinking vaguely that she might need to lend them to some man who might come later to do heavy work about the house or garden, but Q had been wearing his own stout pair of boots. There was a coat, too, still packed away. She had no idea of Ben's foot size, neither did she want the wellingtons thrown back at her.

Later that afternoon, having worn out all means of procrastination, Angela prepared to go down to Gatekeeper's Cottage. Gilles Richard had certainly stirred her emotions in a way that she hadn't experienced for many years. She smiled at the memory of their last meeting. But before she had even zipped up her waterproof, the doorbell rang.

"Now what?" she said to the dog. As she opened the door, she blinked with surprise. "Debs!"

"Hello, Mum."

Her elder daughter dropped an assortment of bags at Angela's feet and swept her into a brief hug, turning her face sideways to receive her mother's welcoming kiss.

"You could have let me know when to expect you." Angela could hear the reproach in her voice. "There's next to nothing in the fridge. I was going to go shopping tomorrow."

Debs shrugged off her coat and threw it over the back of a chair as she followed Angela into the sitting room. She looked around. "This place doesn't look so bad now it's furnished," she remarked.

Angela bit back a sharp retort. For some reason, Debs had been totally against their coming to live in north Cambridgeshire.

"You can't go and bury yourself alive like that," she'd stormed at Angela. "Leave London, leave all your friends."

Leave all my married couple friends, my memories of troubled times, Angela had thought.

"Everyone was really kind when your dad had his accident, but after a while invitations for a single woman stop coming. I need to get away from old associations, start afresh, learn to depend on myself again."

"And what about your literary connections?" Debs had countered.

"There are telephones, the internet," she'd answered. "I can contact my publisher with ease at any time. I can write anywhere."

Then they'd come to the crux of it. "This is our home. It's where we were all together and happy."

"Oh, darling. I do understand that's how you see it, but I've told you, we can't afford to continue living in London. You're not here so much with your studies and everything, anyway."

"Well, what about Grace?" Debs had been ruthless. "Is it fair to drag her off to some godforsaken hole in the country?"

That had really stung, but Grace had flown to Angela's defence.

"I'm happy to go. I like the countryside. Mum and I have agreed that's what we're doing, so stop badgering her."

There had been an atmosphere in the family home for considerably longer than usual after that little scene.

Now, Debs said carelessly, "Don't bother about feeding me. I'm not hungry, anyway. If you've got some eggs, I'll have an omelette for lunch."

"It's early closing at the shop down the road, but if I hurry I'll get there before Miss Brooks shuts." Angela seized a shopping bag. "We must have some vegetables and maybe fruit for suppertime."

There was a queue in the store and Miss Brooks was flustered and irritable. Angela looked around, awaiting her turn. She cheerfully answered one or two queries as to how she and Grace were settling in. When she returned to Slater's Cottage, Debs was gazing at a large square box of summer bedding plants, all in flower.

"How marvellous, but where did you conjure those from?" Angela beamed at her.

"Oh, they're not mine. A man just brought them. He was going to leave them on the doorstep by the look of it, but I spotted him from the window."

"Man? Was he a French man?"

"French? Good grief, no. Local guy, I'd say. Flat cap, straw-coloured hair." Debs gave half a laugh. "When I opened the door, he just stood there, tongue-tied, turning bright pink. I'm sure I saw him as I arrived in the village. He was driving a tractor then. Had a dog in the cab with him. That's why I noticed him. Lovely border collie, like Ranger."

"It must have been Alan Cooper," Angela said, very much surprised. "How kind of him, and very unexpected."

"He almost took them away again when I said you were out, but I told him I'd keep them in until after I've dug over the garden." She gave her mum an odd look. "Mum, you haven't picked up a fancy-man already, have you?" She raised her eyebrows.

"Don't be so silly," Angela said, rather more sharply than she intended. "We'll get them in, but you can't dig over the garden. It's really heavy work. The gardener at the big house has a grandson who has run the cultivator over it — he was coming back to finish it, but he's got measles, of all things."

"Of course I can do it, I'm as strong as a mule. Have to be sometimes, at vet school. Don't fuss, Mum. I'll start after lunch." Debs made for the stairs. Halfway up, she said over her shoulder, "That Alan guy took the cultivator. Said it was his."

"Yes, he lent it to me." Angela stared after her daughter. She was astonished by the farmer's kindness. She hoped the flowers would transplant successfully as late as this. What a lovely start to her garden.

Angela wondered what made him think of doing such a thing. He must have robbed his own garden for hers, though there was no sign of anything as nice at the front of his house. Perhaps he had a back garden that was better.

At the back of her mind she was aware of the faintest disappointment. She could easily have imagined the charming Gilles Richard performing such a kind deed, but bashful, awkward Alan Cooper? She had barely exchanged two sentences with him.

While they ate a lunch of omelettes and salad, Angela questioned Debs about her stay in France. Debs's friends, the Garots, lived in the small town of St André de la Marche, and her daughter showed unusual warmth and enthusiasm describing it.

"It has a shoe museum, of all things, but actually it was quite interesting."

"And the vetting?"

"Oh, I've applied already. To a place not far from here." Debs named a small town in South Lincolnshire. She shot a look at Angela from a under her brows. "If I get it, I can live here for a while, keep an eye on you and Grace."

Angela hoped her face did not betray her feelings. She couldn't help wondering how the three of them would find living together without Ade's ameliorating influence. He had always seemed to understand Debs better than she did.

"That would be lovely, darling," she said. It sounded lame even to herself.

"Well, I'd better get going outside," Debs said briskly, ignoring another half protest from her mother. Angela watched her from the window as she marched across the garden, spade and fork in hand, before she retired to her tiny study and tried, unsuccessfully, to write a short piece entitled 'Starting Your Garden From Scratch'. She had earmarked a magazine which might take it. Writing an article might be one way of getting back into the writing habit. Visiting Gilles Richard was postponed, she realised with semi-relief. Well, she couldn't leave Debs working so hard when she'd only just arrived, could she?

When Grace arrived home from school, the long stretch of garden was already a quarter dug. Debs came in looking hot.

The sisters greeted each other affectionately. Despite the difference in their ages, they usually got on well, although tiffs could blow up in seconds. Grace was not quelled by what she termed Debs's bossiness, as Angela often was.

"Any chance of a hot bath?" Debs asked.

Grace answered airily, "Of course, even this 'godforsaken hole' has hot water."

Angela noticed Debs's lips straighten, and she shot a warning glance at her younger daughter. Having been thwarted in her mission to visit Q Richard earlier, she diverted a bickering session now by saying, "After supper, I'll walk down to Gatekeeper's Cottage and ask how Q Richard is getting along.

Want to come, either of you? I'll call at Home Farm, too, and thank Alan Cooper for the plants."

"Can't," Grace said. "I've got a history thing to do by Friday. Honestly, I do think old Squeers is mean to give it to us so near the end of term."

Squeers was the student's nickname for the history teacher who, Angela gathered, was universally unpopular.

"I'll come," Debs said. "I suppose I'd better start getting to know the locals."

Angela's head swivelled, but she managed to avoid a comment. Debs had used the kind of disdainful tone that Angela disliked. She knew Debs was no snob but often covered her lack of confidence with an air of superiority that could be entirely misleading.

"Good," she said breezily.

When Alan Cooper opened the door to them, they saw at once that he was agitated. His sleeves were rolled up above the elbows, his face was brick-red, and his straw hair stood upright, as though rumpled by worried fingers. He gaped at the sight of the two women.

"We've just called to say thank you for the bedding plants," Angela said. "So very kind and thoughtful of you."

Alan Cooper turned, if possible, even redder. "No trouble ... thought you might like them... Can't stand talking. I've a cow in labour and she's having trouble. I was just about to phone the vet."

It was the longest speech Angela had so far heard him utter. Before she could express concern, Debs said, "I'm a qualified vet, now. Perhaps I can help? What seems to be the matter?"

His face became animated. "Well, I don't know..." he began, but Debs already had her cardigan off, passing it to Angela.

"I'm sure she's competent." Angela spoke to Alan's back as she followed them round the house and out to the barn, unsure what else to do.

It was a dark, cavernous area with meagre electric light. The smell of manure and warm cow was overpowering in the enclosed space. Angela stood with arms folded and shuffled her feet.

As she stood, she heard the words 'uterine torsion' and 'big calf' and, deciding it was not for her, sidled out, leaving Debs to complete her task. She was already oblivious to her mother's presence anyway, and seemed immune to the bleak space.

Angela walked the short way to Gatekeeper's Cottage, now alone and nervous. She could not prevaricate further.

CHAPTER 8

It was a fine summer's evening. Gilles had to get home to see to Q, but when he saw Harry, the concierge of Moondreams House, he decided to walk down the drive to greet him. There were cars parked and the place still looked crowded. Several couples were walking around the house towards the ballroom. There must be a dance class about to begin. The front door stood open, so maybe the teashop, Tea and Sweet Dreams, was still open, too. Two men were fishing from a rowing boat in the middle of the lake. Gilles Richard spoke with Harry, whom he liked and was pleased to call a friend. From the corner of his eye, he spotted Angela and saw her hesitate as she approached, so he made his farewells.

He moved towards her and smiled. "Mrs Ross, good evening. You are quite well settled in your house?"

"Thank you, yes. I've come to enquire after Q."

"But that is most kind. The poor lad is quite ill, I think. This one can be virulent when it is caught by an older person, not a child. I do not like to leave him, but I have my duties to perform."

"Of course. Er, do you think he would mind if I called in to see him? I've had measles, and my daughters have been immunisedagainst it."

Gilles guessed she was asking if *he* minded and was trying to be tactful about his capabilities. He'd come across these strategies before from women trying to look after him and Q. When his wife had died, there had been several well-meaning gifts at his door — usually an apple pie or a casserole. Now, he gave Angela his most engaging smile. "*I* should be pleased for you to visit, and I'm sure Q would appreciate it too." He was rewarded with a delightful pink flush that crept up her neck and across her cheeks. "As you see, much is happening here." He waved his hand. "I should be most grateful. Q is probably in the living room, where we sat before. Please, tell him I shall return as soon as it is possible."

He watched her go and admired her slim waist and the swing of her hips.

Angela entered the cottage and cautiously called, "Q? Hello. It's Angela, Grace's mum. I spoke to your grandfather. Hello? May I come in?"

She edged along the hallway and knocked on the kitchen door at the end. "Hello?" She pushed the door until the opening was wide enough for her to peep around, noting that even under present circumstances the house looked clean and smelled of beeswax polish. Perhaps Gilles had a cleaning lady, or a friend who came and spent time doing such jobs. She recognised a shiver of jealousy and chided herself. Q sat in one of the chairs next to the ancient range. He raised his head and peered at her with a muffled, "Hi."

"It's Angela Ross, Grace's mum. May I come in?"

The boy looked at her with fever-bright eyes. His face and neck were smothered in a thick double rash.

"Hello, Q. I'm sorry you're ill. Is there anything I can do for you?" She glanced around. "I see you've got water." A bottle was left within reach, but a jug that appeared to have contained squash, covered with a clean linen cloth, was now almost empty.

"I'm so thirsty," Q mumbled, moving his head restlessly.

"I'll fetch more squash."

Angela took the jug across to the sink, rinsed it out and mixed some more. She handed the boy a glass and he gulped the liquid. He looked damp with sweat.

"The light's so bright," he said.

She pulled the curtains half across. "Keep it like that and then your eyes won't ache." She considered for a moment. "I think you'll be much more comfortable if you have a sponge wash around your face and neck," she said.

He was only half awake, much too ill to protest. Angela found a bowl in a cupboard, filled it with lukewarm water, found a sponge and towel in the bathroom, and left them at the sink before helping Q to stand and walk across the room.

"I'll be back in a minute." *Lanky as a half-grown colt*, she thought as she went outside to give him some space and privacy.

When she returned, she again knocked on the door before entering the kitchen. "Now, does that feel a little better, Q?"

"Yes, thanks. Where is *Grandpère*?"

"He'll be here soon. I saw him on the driveway near the house. It's busy, but it'll soon quieten down. The fishermen in their boat will be mooring up for the night, and I imagine your grandfather's work for the day will be done. Grace sends you her best wishes and I have these *Digest* magazines. I'll leave them here by your chair. I don't know if you would like them but when you feel better, they may interest you."

She was drying the basin when Gilles came into the kitchen, asking immediately, "How is the boy?"

"He is rather ill," Angela said, but then turning to Q she added, "but you'll recover soon."

"Grace's mum has been very kind," Q muttered, and he told Gilles what she had done.

"You may need to keep the curtains pulled across the window, and he needs to stay warm. There is a risk of complications to the eyes and chest with measles. Please, I'm not trying to interfere."

Gilles noticed the sudden confusion cross her face.

"Did he not have an inoculation against it when he was small?"

He spread his arms and shrugged. "I don't know, *Madame*. My daughter and then my wife attended to such matters concerning the boy's health."

"I think I'll go back to bed now," Q said.

Gilles helped him up.

"I better go." Angela picked up her bag.

Gilles indicated the empty chair. "Please sit and take a glass of wine with me?"

Twilight was starting to dim the room and he saw her hesitate. "Please. It would be good to talk. I believe we have some shared experiences. I should be honoured if you would join me for one glass. I'll be back in a minute." He escorted the boy from the room, giving her no time to argue.

When Gilles returned five minutes later, he said, "You understand it was not always easy, bringing up someone else's child. My daughter, Bettine, died when Q was only small. She ailed for some years before she died. And since my wife also died…"

"Yes, it must be difficult." He saw Angela's eyes sparkle with moisture and was aware of a lump in his own throat.

"At times." He tried to be honest without frightening her away. He could see she was anxious, but he so wanted to get to know her better. "Q is a good boy." Gilles fetched a bottle of white wine and poured some into two glasses he took from the dresser shelf. "Well, I think he is a good boy, but he has a wilful streak and I know some others think him wild. It is in his nature. In school he is sometimes in trouble because he will not work as he should. I've had to go there to see his teachers. He is rude sometimes and answers back." He shook his head and passed her a glass. "That is most unacceptable."

Angela took a sip of the cool, crisp wine. It soothed her, and she took a deep breath. "He has been polite to me at all times. I dare say many boys can be a little wild at this age. He has been growing up and finding his feet, perhaps over-compensating," she said. "His mother died when he was very young and then he lost his mother at a sensitive age. Or perhaps it's because he doesn't know yet what he wishes to do with his life, so he has no strong incentive."

Gilles nodded. "Maybe that is the reason," he said. "But he must work. He must gain qualifications to keep himself. Later, perhaps, a wife and children."

"At Q's age, they seldom consider the future."

"I have tried talking with him, but he shrugs. He says he will manage. It is a great worry."

"I'm sure it must be."

Gilles regarded her. There was warm sympathy in her eyes as she leaned towards him.

"Maybe girls are easier to bring up than boys. I don't know. Debs, my older daughter, has always been quite ambitious to do well, although she and I don't always see eye to eye. She always got on better with my husband, so I understand how hard it can be. Grace is more easy-going and gets good school reports."

Gilles shook his head and sighed. He stood to retrieve the bottle from the table, topped up her glass and switched on a lamp. A pool of light fell on Angela's dark, glossy hair and shone from her crown.

"I think Q misses my wife, his grandmother, very much, though he does not speak of her. It is since she died that he became wild, always riding out on his motorcycle, talking impolitely to his teachers."

"My husband, Ade, had a motorcycle accident. It was in London, where it is so much busier. Someone came from a sideroad in a large van, and he was killed instantly."

Gilles paused before responding to this information, which he had already gleaned from people in the village. "I see. You must have been a happy family until then."

"Well..." He heard the hesitation in her voice. "Yes, I suppose so. Well, sort of. Actually, I don't know." He watched her take a gulp of wine before placing her glass on the floor by her feet.

"If you wish to tell me, I am a good listener," he said. "Whatever you say here will be safe with me." He leaned forward to encourage her. "And please, you must call me Gilles if we are to be neighbours and good friends."

"And I am Angela." She gave a self-conscious smile and mirrored his movement, supporting her head on her hands.

Suddenly, she seemed unable to stop it all tumbling out. The image of Ade with a woman; his passing before she could ask him for an explanation; her image of herself, being less than a good wife should be; her guilt over her doubts.

Perhaps it was the wine, the dim light in the kitchen, or him being a comparative stranger. In the telling, she let him see her insecurity and lack of self-worth. It wrung his heart that anyone should feel that way. He wanted to enfold her in his arms and take away her confusion, but he stayed still and silent.

After what seemed an age, he spoke quietly. "I understand. When my wife died — I would have taken away her pain if I could. I suffered guilt for not being able to do that. More recently, I have begun to understand that hanging onto those emotions does nothing. Perhaps I am too lazy." He gave a disparaging, mirthless laugh and she looked up at him. Then he reached out to her, and she took his hands.

"Too lazy?"

"It was hard work, those feelings. I decided I must let them go if I was to have the energy to carry on. They are too much like leeches, you know? They will empty you until you have nothing left to give anyone. You must respect yourself, Angelique. Have faith in your own value. You have survived. I think you are a proud person, but your family will help you to carry on, if you let them." Then he added, quietly, "As will your friends."

He could see tears threatening to spill over. She gave a watery smile.

"Thank you," she whispered. She withdrew her hands and dashed one against her eyes, then dug up her sleeve to produce a tissue with which she wiped her nose. "Listen to me going on." She smiled. "I came to help you and Q, and you've ended up guiding me. Oh, my goodness, I must be going." She gulped the last of her wine and leaped up.

"I shall accompany you to the end of the lane," Gilles said.

"No need. Really, I'll be fine."

"I'll just tell Q."

When he came down, she had left the house and was already several yards away. He sprinted to catch up. She walked with her arms folded.

"Please do not feel awkward for what you have shared with me," he said, trying to sound reassuring.

Silence stretched between them as they marched on. At the junction of the lane and the road into the village, she said, "Thank you. It's only a few yards from here."

"Please call again. Come in the morning, if you wish. Q would be pleased to see you."

He stood still as she walked away, noticing the stiff squareness of her shoulders.

As would I, he thought as he watched.

CHAPTER 9

As she walked away, Angela was aware that Gilles watched her. She stiffened her back and looked ahead. How could she have been so embarrassingly open with him? She had thought him autocratic when they'd first met, and now he'd revealed that he was out of his depth, trying to guide a strong-willed teenage boy single-handed. He'd also let her know he had struggled after his wife died. He rolled his 'r' sounds and pronounced many words in such an attractive way. She was foolishly flustered.

When she reached her little gate, she stole a glance and caught his figure retreating around the corner. He had watched her to her gate, although she had told him she was fine to walk the last bit on her own. Surely that said something about him.

She didn't see Debs until the next morning, after Grace had left to catch the bus. She'd been vaguely aware of the sound of the front door after she had gone to bed.

"How did things go yesterday, with the cow?" she asked after breakfast, when her daughter emerged.

"Oh, at Alan's? Fine in the end. It's a heifer, which for Alan is better than a bull calf, economically. Its forelegs were bent under, but we managed to free them. It took quite a while."

"You were late home. It must have been difficult."

"It took a while, and it's hard work so Alan asked me in for a bite to eat and a beer when we'd finished," Debs said.

Angela knew better than to comment, and anyway Debs was busying herself at the dishwasher to avoid eye contact. It would have been lovely to speak with her daughter about how she felt, but that wasn't going to happen.

Angela decided to take the bull by the horns, so to speak, and call on Q and Gilles again. After all, he had invited her to do so, and she couldn't avoid him because of her own misgivings about divulging her business the previous evening.

As Angela left the house, she noticed the girls had heeled in the flowers that Alan Cooper had given them. Although they looked droopy in their home under the windows, they would probably survive and add some colour soon, if she kept them well-watered.

When she arrived at Gatekeeper's Cottage, Gilles was just leaving.

"Please go on in. Q will be pleased to see you," he said. "I'm sorry, I cannot stop. I have a delivery to accept. Some large shrubs for a new bed down by the lake."

"No, you must go. I shan't stay long. I brought some sponge cakes that I made yesterday."

"That is kind. I cook, but not dainty cakes." He smiled, and radiance filled Angela. Everything would be all right. There was no more awkwardness. She smiled back at him and headed for the open doorway.

After spending time chatting with Q and replenishing his jug of squash, she thought, *Gilles better be careful. The boy is polite and pleasantly confident. He's so worried the lad will go off the rails, but he'll drive him there if he pushes too hard.* She was exceptionally lucky with Grace and although Debs was so touchy, at least her career was going well. Despite all their own apparent troubles, Ade had always been there for his children, especially Debs. For that she had to be grateful.

She found a plate on the dresser in the kitchen and was arranging the cakes and chattering to Q when she heard the front door open and close. She stopped her task and looked up as Gilles entered. His presence made the room seem small, and once more she experienced a curious mix of awkwardness and excitement at the sight of him.

"You will take a coffee?" As soon as he spoke, she relaxed.

"Thank you, but I mustn't stay long."

Her eyes followed his frame as he moved easily about the kitchen, gathering what he needed and making their drinks.

He was so different to the husband she had known so intimately. Ade had only been half a head taller than she. His stocky build had been a comfort to her in her younger years, and his square hands had been capable. He bothered about his appearance, wearing clothes that spoke of money and maintaining good grooming. His hair was always artfully mussed to give the appearance of careless class, but she knew he spent plenty on a good cut and products to keep it in place.

This man was tall and rangy, with long-fingered hands. His jeans hung on his slim hips and his shirt, though very white, was partially untucked. His hair curled onto his collar. His eyes were dark but sparked with a penetrating glow. It was a long time, she realised, since she had been gazed at like that.

"I think you take it in the English way? Weak and perhaps with milk?" he enquired. "We like it so strong that the spoon might stand upright." He laughed and Angela was brought back to reality.

There was no further intimate divulgence of feelings from either of them. They spoke of the garden, the weather, Gilles's work around the estate and greenhouses, and his plans for the parterre, but they avoided discussing their children. Angela confessed that she wrote for a living.

"Not that it earns a huge amount," she said, "but it's enough to mean we don't starve. I am lucky that the house in London sold for such a good price. Living here is much cheaper and the insurance money helps too, of course. I have to be practical about that."

"Of course," he answered mildly. "It is the same for me. The world continues to turn." He shrugged in that oh-so-French way that was distinctly attractive.

"I must go," Angela said. She laughed nervously. "I've some flowers that Alan Cooper gave us that need watering."

She was unprepared for the change that came over Gilles.

"Flowers?" he snapped. "Alan, he gives you flowers?"

"Plants," she corrected. "Only some bedding plants for the garden."

"*Tiens!* So, he gives you a present already?"

"Why not? It was kind of him." Feeling a mix of surprise, amusement, and irritation, Angela turned for the door. "Goodbye, Gilles. I'll visit Q again, if I may?"

She slipped out into the sunshine and heard his faint reply: "*Au revoir*, Angelique."

As she wandered along the lane and headed for home, she had plenty to think about. Why had he been so irritated by the thought of Alan Cooper donating a few flowers for her new garden?

CHAPTER 10

"How do you suppose Q is?" Grace wanted to know. It was the day after the end of term, and she was preparing to take Ranger for a walk. "I'm sick of the same old way past the woods to the quarry. I might go a different way. Along the river, maybe."

She knew perfectly well she was hoping for an accidental encounter with the gardener's grandson. Her mum probably knew it too, although she made no mention of that.

Grace crossed the fields and walked down to the old mill by the footpath before wandering along the river bank. She'd had no news of Q for three days, for her mother had stopped her daily visits now the boy's health had improved. Angela's ministrations had broadened to include the taking of homemade chicken broth, but three days ago she had found Q up and dressed in the kitchen.

"Really, Mum, people will begin to think you are trying to entice Gilles Richard with all your homemade goodies," Debs had said.

"What utter nonsense." Her mother's response was sharp, and Grace looked at Debs, barely repressing a snigger.

Angela had decided she must not do any more. It made her seem needy for friendship, and she was embarrassed by the thought. She had said as much to Grace in a moment of openness. She had come home on that last occasion and remarked to the girls, "I really can't afford to neglect my writing any more if we're to have jam on our bread."

It was a Friday when Grace took her walk, so there were only one or two people on the river bank as she rounded the mill and came in sight of the Gatekeeper's Cottage. She saw Q at once, sitting on a bench, idly throwing pebbles into a tin. Grace went forwards slowly, ill at ease, and almost wishing she hadn't chosen to go that way. Q looked pale, the faded rash showing blue under his olive skin. The moment he saw her, his bored expression changed to a delighted smile.

Grace smiled back. "Hey."

"Hi there," he said.

"How're you feeling now?"

"Not so bad, thanks. Just a bit washed out." He leaned forwards to rub Ranger's ears. "Stupid to catch measles. A kid's illness." He looked at Grace sideways.

"Anyone can catch it at any age." She perched on the end of the bench.

"You've cut your hair. Suits you, sort of curly like that," he said, avoiding her eyes.

She touched it self-consciously. "Thanks. My mum's a bit cross about it. She liked it long."

"It's *your* hair. You can do what you want with it."

"Mm."

"Your mum's been really good, coming to see me each day. She brought some great stuff, too. Thanks for the magazines, by the way. Saved me from going mad with boredom." He paused, then added, "Sorry I didn't get your garden finished."

"Debs, my sister, has come home. She dug the garden, and Mr Cooper from Home Farm gave Mum a huge box of summer bedding plants."

Q gave a snort of laughter.

"What's so funny?" Grace asked.

"*Grandpère* was a bit peeved about that," he told her. "I reckon he wished he'd thought of doing it first."

71

Grace was startled, and Q must have noticed the frown of puzzlement, for he changed the subject hastily.

"Is your sister going to stay with you now?"

"Could be, but she'll have to get a vet's job. She's been on a work experience thing in France before coming here. She finished university before that."

"Where's she been in France?"

"The twinning place near the Loire. St André de la Marche, is it?"

He chortled.

"What?"

"Your accent. It's so … English."

"What do you expect? I *am* English."

"And good Lord, that's where we used to live. I suppose that's why we ended up here. The twinning thing. It's a bigger place than this, though."

"Really?" Grace's interest was tickled. "It's a sort of fishing, farming place, isn't it?"

"Uh-huh. *Grandpère* was in the French merchant navy then. He used to travel to St Nazaire to join ships. That was only a couple of hours away. But it was ages ago, when I was a child. I can't remember it. We came here when I was only five."

"Haven't you ever been back?" Grace asked. "For a holiday or to visit friends?"

"No." Q looked away down the drive towards the big house to where a coppice of aspens shimmered in the sunlight. "*Grandpère* won't go." Grace thought he sounded reluctant. "He um … won't even talk about the place."

"Perhaps your grandparents weren't happy living there," Grace suggested.

"I remember *Mémé* saying they were. She liked it." He gave Grace a swift look.

"Is that what you called your granny in French?"

"Mm. My surname's not actually Richard, you know."

"Isn't it?"

"Well, if it was, it would mean my parents weren't married, wouldn't it?" He sounded nonchalant. "My mother was *Grandpère's* daughter."

"Oh." Grace hadn't given the matter any thought and now was nonplussed, unsure what he expected her to say.

"My name's really Bruno Qu'appelle Richard-Something," Q announced, then grinned. "But I don't know what the 'something' is. It's a bit of a mouthful, isn't it?"

Grace laughed. "Quite a bit."

"I asked *Grandpère* about it some time ago, soon after *Mémé* died." Q's tone was casual. "Why he wants me called Q Richard, and I asked what my real name is."

"What did he say?" Grace was fast becoming intrigued.

"He got annoyed," said Q. "First, he wanted to know who told me about it all, so I told him I'd asked *Mémé*. He said she'd had no business to tell me, but I thought my parents probably weren't married. Not that it matters." Airily he went on, "She said that wasn't it, but she wouldn't speak of my father. When we came to England, *Grandpère* thought it would be much easier if we all had the same name, Richard."

"Was your mother known as Mrs Richard here, then?"

Q nodded.

There was a pause before Grace asked tentatively, "So what happened to your father?"

"Haven't a clue," Q said with an air of bravado. "*Grandpère* refuses to talk about him. Some villain who just left us when I was a kid, I suppose."

"Maybe," Grace agreed with caution.

Barely seems a sufficient reason for the whole Richard family to have packed up and emigrated here, she thought.

After a moment, Q looked anxious and said, "I've been rabbiting on, haven't I? Dunno why I told you all that. I ... I'd rather you kept it to yourself. I mean, I don't want Milly Paige or that bloody Tracey Sutton and the rest chattering about it."

"Of course. I won't tell anyone." She was wickedly delighted as she contemplated what he had just said about Tracey.

"I dare say people in the village *may* know," Q said. "The older lot here. But they may have forgotten. It's ten years since *Maman* died."

"I shan't tell," Grace repeated.

"Thanks." Q gazed down at the river. "I wish *Grandpère* wouldn't be so cagey. After all, it's my father, and now there's no one else I can ask about it. Since I don't know his name, I can't even Google him. I think I've a right to know. Don't you agree?"

"Well ... yes, I do," Grace said. "But if it upsets your grandad to talk about him, perhaps he'll explain later on."

"Later on?" Q's voice rose. "Dammit, I'm seventeen. What do you mean, later on?"

"I ... I just mean, well, sometime, when you're completely grown up and maybe ready to leave here."

Q glowered at her in silence, so she got up.

"Think I'd better be going home now. Come on, Ranger."

The boy leaped to his feet. "Oh, don't go. Please. Sorry I snapped at you. I'm sick of my own company. Er ... do you play Xbox or something?"

"Depends what game. Not very well. Debs usually beats me."

"I'm no champion either, but let's go into the house and play something, shall we? Go on, say you will."

Grace hesitated. "All right then, but I'll have to text my mum to tell her where I am." She dug her phone from her back pocket. "Where's your grandad?"

"Gone into Peterborough. He'll be back at teatime. It's okay to come on in, though."

"What about Ranger?"

"He better not come in the house, but he can't escape from the garden. He'll be okay outside. I'll give him some water."

She followed him into the house and looked around as she went into a kitchen which seemed to double as a dining room. They sat at the table, and he switched on the TV screen and Xbox.

They played Forza Motorsport. He won the first round easily, but he gave her some tips on how to improve her game. Grace soon showed skill with it, so they decided on the best of three. Grace drew the line at the FIFA game, so Q dug out a Lego Batman quest from the bottom of the pile and they laughed a lot as they completed the missions and found their way around. They ate ham sandwiches, hastily made by Q, and shared a big bottle of cola. By mid-afternoon, they knew a lot about each other.

Grace learned that Q was only continuing with sixth form to please his grandfather. He longed to travel. Grace wanted to see the world, but she had promised her mother to aim for a place at university first. "After I've done that, I can go anywhere, and I'll always have something to fall back on. I'll only be twenty-one or -two by the time I graduate. I think I'd like to teach," she told Q. "Not in England, though. Somewhere abroad. Maybe Canada or Australia, but that would mean leaving Mum on her own and I know I'd feel guilty."

"It's your life, though," Q protested. "Your mother shouldn't hold you back."

"She wouldn't," flashed Grace. "Only I know she'd be lonely on her own, now Dad's gone."

"There's your sister," the boy began, but Grace shook her head.

"Mum and Debs don't get on that well, and Debs has her own work. She's fully qualified now, so she'll get a job as a vet."

"Well, it's a long time off yet. Things can change. What subject would you teach?"

"History, I think."

"History! How boring can you get?"

"It doesn't have to be boring," Grace said and stuck her chin out.

"Then I'll have to call you Mrs Squeers."

"Q Richard, don't you dare."

So, they ended the afternoon by laughing and teasing each other and inventing absurd nicknames for the rest of the teachers in the school.

Grace gathered Ranger from his sleep in the sun on the front step and headed home. Her thoughts turned to her mother after the conversation with Q about their future aspirations.

She remembered one awful row she had half overheard between her parents not long before her dad had died. It had disturbed her to the extent she hadn't told anyone. Not Debs, not even Gemma, her best friend at her previous school, and they normally shared everything. When she thought about it, her parents had either been distant with each other for a while before that great argument or they had niggled and bickered. They didn't hug each other anymore or speak with affectionate teasing. During the row, her father had called her mother stupid. She'd heard him shout that word and it had shocked her. It had ended with him banging out of the house. Less than a week later he was dead, under the wheels of a van.

She hadn't told her mum about her recurring nightmare, either. She could remember running and tripping over, and when she got up, all her teeth had fallen out. It might have been funny if she hadn't been so terrified. On her own in hot and tangled sheets, she awoke in a sweat, breathless. The bedclothes clawed at her body as she sat up and tried to rid herself of the fear.

She'd looked it up on the internet after she'd had the same dream for the third time. It was not uncommon, the teeth thing, apparently. That surprised her. *These dreams are typically associated with feelings of powerlessness and loss of control,* she read. *They might occur at times of transition. Sometimes such dreams indicate the loss of something or someone important. A further explanation can be a lack of self-worth and feelings of insecurity.*

After Grace had read this, she decided not to share that with anyone either, especially her mother. It sounded like a load of rubbish anyway. Her mum had enough to worry about. She still had the dream sometimes, although not as often.

It must've been lonely for Mum, she thought, *although Dad was out a lot just before he died, anyway. Mum said he was busy at work.*

CHAPTER 11

Q and Grace hauled the little boat further up onto the bank of the lake as Gilles stood outside Moondreams House with the wheelbarrow and tools for digging, watching them. He turned as the owner, David, approached.

"Just taking a break," he said. "Watching those two. I hope it is all right for them to use your lake like this."

"Oh, yes. They'll take care of things, and Q lives here. Can't let all the local teenagers congregate, but they're fine. Is that the new girl in the village?"

"Yes, the daughter of Angela, who has moved into Slater's Cottage. Her name is Grace. A good influence, I think." He felt warmth inside his chest at the sight of the lad being enthusiastic about something so innocent. For so long, he had worried about the direction Q was taking. His rudeness and lack of enthusiasm at school; his wild riding of the bike, to the extent that he got a speeding ticket; the way he rolled his eyes when they crossed verbal swords. All these things, and no one for Gilles to discuss it with or receive advice from, since his wife died. He was always analysing what he did and the responses he gave the boy, wondering if he, himself, was the cause of the difficulties they were both experiencing. So, to see him so engaged was both a relief and a joy.

"Right. How is the new shrubbery coming along?"

They talked about that, before David left and Gilles lifted the handles of the barrow as he thought about his grandson.

That morning, Q had asked him if they could do up the little boat. As Gilles agreed, Q already had his phone out, and was heard speaking to Grace as he took the stairs, two at a time, to the privacy of his own bedroom.

When he came down again with a grin on his face, Gilles said, "The outboard may be *kaput*. It is so ancient. You'll have to strip it down. At least because it is old you will be able to do that. Not like these new things that are all computerised and have integral parts."

So, there they were, Q and Grace. As he watched, they were clearly deliberating over how to proceed. The warmth of pride in his grandson satisfied him. As he approached, he heard Q directing the process as he stood stroking his chin, gesticulating at various parts of the small craft. Gilles's mouth twitched at the sight.

Not many weeks ago, Q had been tearing down the A1 on his motorbike, from what he'd learned when the police had called. That time it was a friendly warning, if such conversations could ever be friendly. Still, he had been extremely grateful for the intervention. As soon as they had left, and Gilles had tried to speak calmly, Q had raised his eyes and stormed from the room.

Now he smiled and raised his hand in greeting as Grace turned and saw him watching. She approached.

"I think we need sandpaper. Two types, Q said." She relayed the lad's request. Gilles was quietly impressed with Q's perception. Something must have sunk in from the activities they had shared over the years.

"Come into the house. I'll see what I can find; there's some stuff down in the cellar." She followed him as he lifted the latch of the oak door, switched on the light, and ducked his head as he descended the stone steps.

"How come it's dry in here? We must be below the water level," Grace said.

"Sometimes in winter we must pump it out, but in summer it's okay. All the things I keep down here are in plastic boxes on shelves, so they don't get damp. It smells a little musty, but it's fine for these things."

She waited on the steps while he found what he was looking for.

He turned with a box in his hands, and they went back to the kitchen, where he placed it on the table.

"This is what you'll need. Now, the grain of a wood is the direction in which most of the wood fibres are pointing, and one of the main things in woodworking is to sand with the grain. That might be tricky sometimes, but it's important to avoid sanding across the grain. Sanding against the grain leaves scratches. That defeats the purpose of sanding the wood."

"Oh, I know, *Capitaine* Richard. Q explained that to me already. He knows what he's doing. You don't need to worry."

"Right," Gilles said, and managed to avoid a grin. "Call me Gilles, though. Not so formal if we are all to be friends."

When he left to return to his work, Grace was busy sanding and Q had a spanner in his hands and was stripping down the outboard motor. When he returned a couple of hours later, they were still at it, although a bottle of Coke and two mugs lay on the grass beside them.

Each day they worked from early morning until dusk, and Grace was soon as tanned as the boy, living in shorts and T-shirts. Gilles continued to take pleasure in seeing them enjoy the task.

"It's time wasted, all this taking the bike into Peterborough when I need a spare part," Q said, one morning at breakfast.

Gilles said nothing more than a cursory, "Mm," but he noted the reluctance that Q had to taking his motorbike out of the shed.

It was a proud moment when Grace added a final flourish to the last letter of the boat's name — *French Miss*.

Angela, Debs and Gilles were invited to the launch a few days later, but at the last minute, Debs had to work. She had got the veterinary job she had applied for and had begun travelling to the Deepings in her small car. So it was that Angela walked up the drive towards Moondreams House and across the front, where she had arranged to meet Gilles.

Annie, who ran the dance school in the ballroom of Moondreams House, was heading that way, too. Angela had met her once or twice around the village and had learned that she was married to Harry, and they had a baby daughter named Evie. "Hello," Angela greeted, and explained that she was waiting for Gilles. "We've had a formal invitation from Q and my daughter, Grace. They're launching the little boat they've been working on."

"I've seen them down there most days." Annie smiled. "Evie and I were having a toddle by the lake a couple of days ago and they were hard at it."

"How is Evie? She looked so adorable when I saw you at the shop the other day," Angela said.

"She is adorable, of course, but it's also the terrible twos so she has her moments. Harry's doing the bath routine tonight because I'm teaching one of my dance classes. He can have the hair wash fight." Annie laughed.

"I remember it well, even though it was a long time ago for me. Oh, there's Gilles coming."

"And I mustn't be late for my beginners' class. They only started a couple of weeks ago, so they're all really keen. They'll be beating down the door at this rate. See you soon. Enjoy your launch ceremony."

Angela watched her go as she waited for Gilles to catch up with her, and when he did she said, "Annie seems really nice."

"She is, and a good friend for you, if ever you need one, as Harry is for me. Are you ready for this?" He nodded towards the lake.

Gilles and Angela stood together on the bank to watch Grace pour a glass of wine over the bow before she and Q heaved and pushed their small craft.

"I'm not breaking a bottle and damaging my paintwork," Grace said.

"Or wasting our wine." Angela laughed and held up her glass towards them.

There was a small backwash as the boat slithered down the bank into the water. The irises at the edge bobbed their yellow heads and a moorhen scooted out from the reeds nearby. A small cloud of flies hovered over some duckweed that had accumulated in a quiet patch without current.

CHAPTER 12

Gilles looked down at Angela's face. The sun shone down on her, giving her hair a healthy shine, and her lips parted as she watched the youngsters. His heart pumped a little harder and he cleared his throat as he bent down to wipe an imaginary mark from the knee of his jeans. As he straightened, foolishness swept through him.

"...them occupied for the first two weeks of the summer." Gilles was suddenly aware that Angela was speaking.

"Sorry? Oh, oh, yes. Every day they have been busy, and now they have their picnic there with them, so I imagine we shan't see them until evening."

"Yes, when the food runs out and they want more." Angela smiled up at him. "Grace loves to be outdoors. It's so good for her here. She has the woods and the quarry to walk the dog, and the summer by this lake is a wonderful opportunity for her to grow away from all the heartache and anxiety of the last year."

"Your daughter is a lovely girl, Angelique. I think she makes a fine companion for the boy. A good influence. She is polite and hard-working. I have seen a difference in Q since they have been friends. This occupation of theirs is youthful and innocent, I believe. It is excellent to see him so happy." Angela said nothing, so he added, "I've spoken to Q and told him he must take the greatest care of her or answer to me."

"I'm sure that he will."

"You do not object to this close friendship that seems to be developing between them?"

"I think, *Capitaine…*"

"Gilles."

"Gilles, I think that you've brought up your grandson well, and taught him good manners and sensible values. And I have tried to do the same with my daughters. Then we can do no more except trust them to behave with responsibility."

"Well, my daughter was maybe not so sensible…" Gilles stopped and changed the subject with speed. "I know of a good place. It is an old mill that has been converted into a restaurant. I haven't been there for a long time, but I hear it is still the place for a treat. It is a few miles from here, on the river, of course, and there are swans. The mill wheel has been preserved and still turns behind the glass. You can witness this from your table. Will you allow me to take you there for dinner one evening soon? Next week, perhaps. I will arrange for someone to stand in for me and do any emergency work here, although that is unlikely to be necessary. Harry would do that." He was aware he was talking too much and stopped.

"Well, I, er…"

"I haven't thanked you properly for your kindness to Q when he was ill. The place is some distance from here, so no one will know that we dine together. No gossips to spread false talk." He grinned. "There is no commitment. A friendly meal."

Angela glanced up at him. He sensed a little panic in her expression, but then her face relaxed. "A friendly meal. No harm in that. Thank you. I'd like that."

They began moving from the bank of the lake. He took her elbow to guide her up the slope.

"Excellent. Then I shall arrange it. Thursday, perhaps, if that is also suitable for you."

"Thursday? Yes, that should be all right. Debs should be home to keep Grace company."

"I am most happy," Gilles stated and gave a small bow as they parted. He was aware that this was probably quaint and old-fashioned, but he didn't care. In that moment, as he watched her walk away, he was more content than he had been in a long while. The lad was absorbed in an innocent activity with a reliable and sensible girl, and now there was the prospect of a sensational dinner partner to look forward to. This latter was something far from his recent experience, and his anticipation was intense.

Gilles and Angela met again much sooner than he expected.

He was breathing hard both with anxiety and his jog through the rain to her porch when the light above came on following his sharp rap, and Angela opened her front door. He batted a moth away from his face.

"I'm really sorry. Can Debs come? Is she at home? I've just had a telephone call from an old man who lives a couple of miles away. His dog has been caught in a rabbit trap and its front paw is most bad. I wouldn't ask, but I wasn't sure what else to do. This poor old chap is crying. His dog is his life."

Debs appeared at Angela's shoulder. "I heard that. What's the address?"

"Oh no, I don't know. I can take you. Would that be all right? The roads are very narrow and it's a long way off the regular route." He looked at Angela.

"Debs, would you like me to come?" she asked her daughter.

"Whatever for? I *can* manage. Perhaps I might follow you, Gilles. Then you could return, and I will come back when I'm ready."

"I don't doubt you can cope," Angela said, "but the roads are so windy and narrow, and it will be pitch-black if it's out in the back of beyond."

"I'll show you the way," Gilles put in. "Thank you so much for coming. I have my car here."

As Gilles sat in his car by the kerb, he fastened the seatbelt and waited for Debs to back out of the driveway. He watched in his mirror for the twin glow of her car's lights as they edged up the village. He could tell Angela was very uneasy about Debs driving along the dark country roads alone. He worried about Q riding his motorbike. It was a parent's lot, no matter how old the child, and he hated the thought of her sitting at home worrying.

The journey was not easy because of the dark and the driving rain. At one point they met a truck coming the other way, and Gilles swore and braked hard. A truck coming that way was ridiculous.

They arrived after a gruelling half hour. Debs got straight on with the job, having retrieved her bag from the back of her car. Gilles followed her to the house and stood to one side, while the old man showed her the problem. There was a copious amount of blood, and tears ran down his crinkled face as he tried to explain what had happened. The dog whimpered but lay in his owner's arms and looked up with trusting eyes, even in its pain.

Gilles tiptoed back to his car and sat inside. He considered going home, but then he thought of the truck and decided to wait. He shivered and switched on the engine for some warmth. It seemed an age before Debs emerged with the old man. He saw them shake hands and she came towards him.

"I'm so sorry. That was quite a long time. You should have gone." She bent to speak to him as he opened his window. "It was a very nasty, deep cut and needed stitching. I'll stop by tomorrow and take another look and change the dressing. It'll be okay."

"Not to worry. I'm glad it was a happy outcome." Gilles climbed out of the car.

"To be honest, I didn't realise you were still waiting. I am grateful. You were correct. It is out in the middle of nowhere."

"It's fine." He smiled at her, noting her anxious face. "If it gives your mother a peaceful mind, it's worth it."

Debs nodded. "I telephoned Peter, who I work with. I can go there. It's closer to here than home. I quite often stay there when it's late."

"I'll follow you there and then go back home."

"I can manage." She repeated what she had said to her mother, but her tone was milder. She smiled and shrugged. "Thank you." She turned for her own car and he climbed back into his.

CHAPTER 13

The vet Debs had joined, Peter Carpenter, in the Deepings —
a cluster of villages in South Lincolnshire — lived on his own
in a large house that adjoined the surgery. When Debs was on
emergency call, he kindly insisted she use his spare room so
that she would be available for telephone calls. This
arrangement seemed to suit everyone. Angela realised it was
good not to have her elder daughter under her roof quite so
much. Debs was happy to semi-move out. When Angela
vaguely questioned the sleeping arrangements, in typical Debs
fashion, she breezed away any suggestion of village chatter and
scoffed at the old-fashioned views elderly clients may have,
adding, "Really, Mother, you sound like a prim old spinster."

"Well, thanks. I simply wondered if he was being thoughtful
about you?"

If Angela had any reservations regarding Grace spending so
much time with Q they were few, but Debs did not share her
mother's reticence.

"Mum, you must be crazy to let her go out with that boy day
after day."

"Grace will behave sensibly."

"Maybe, but what about him? Everyone says he's a tearaway.
You can't think he's a good friend for Grace."

Angela was careful with her reply. "If Q has been wild, I
haven't witnessed it. He doesn't try to avoid coming to the
house to see her. He's always been polite to me. Working on
that boat's been a fun thing for them to do, and now, of
course, they want to make use of it."

Debs made a derisive noise. "I dare say, but I think she spends far too much time on her own with him."

"On a lake with boats and people on the banks?" Angela said lightly, but Debs scowled.

"You know perfectly well what I mean. They seem dotty about each other. Look, I wasn't going to tell you this, but there is definitely something odd about that family, the Richards."

"Odd? What on earth do you mean?"

Debs took a deep breath and sighed. "When I was in St André de la Marche, Jeannette's mother told me she knew of them. It's a bigger place than this, but she'd heard stuff all the same. She spoke of these people who left there and came to live in England, here, in Waterthorpe. When I said that's where you live now, she asked if we knew anyone called Richard, an ex-merchant naval captain and his wife and daughter. The daughter was married and had a child, a boy. I didn't know of them, of course, but after I arrived here, and you introduced me to Gilles Richard, well, it was obvious. Grace says Q told her his family used to live in St André de la Marche. It's all too coincidental."

"Only in as much as St André de la Marche and here are twinned. It seems reasonable for the Richard family to come here as much as anywhere else. After all, you've been there to work and come back here. So, what of all this?" Angela tried to keep the asperity from her voice.

"That's just it. I don't know. *Madame* Garot began telling me there'd been a massive scandal connected to the Richard family but before she could explain, a neighbour called and that was all she got around to telling me."

Angela did not let Debs know that Grace had sworn her to secrecy and repeated Q's confidences about his father, such as they were. She admitted to herself she was puzzled, but she refused to gossip about it. It seemed there must be some sort of mystery attached to Q's father, but she hoped Debs was not going to restart speculation in the village.

"Where is Q's father?" Debs demanded, as if reading her mother's thoughts.

"Perhaps he died. It isn't any of our business, is it?"

"It is if it involves Grace," Debs exploded. "Honestly, you're too soft with her, Mum. Anything she wants to do, you just let her."

"She'll be seventeen next birthday, and I trust her good sense. Besides, if I come down hard she's more likely to rebel and continue seeing Q in secret. At the moment, she's open and honest and I trust her."

"Huh!"

After a moment, Angela said, "If you need reassurance, Gilles Richard has already told me Q promised to look after Grace properly. I think I can trust him too. I like the lad."

"And his grandfather. You're hooked by all that French charm," Debs muttered. "You always trust people far too easily."

"And you, perhaps not easily enough," Angela fired back and left the kitchen to end the conversation.

In spite of her professed belief, the conversation did leave her disturbed. Perhaps one of her new friends might know more — Annie or Pat. Still, she couldn't blurt out the question to people she didn't know well. *Take as you find* was her motto, and that is what she would do. She'd keep her ears and eyes open, though.

After her disagreement with Debs, Angela was feeling increasingly anxious about her impending dinner with Gilles. No commitment? But suppose he took her acceptance as some sort of wish for involvement, despite what he said? And she was in his debt now, for the good deed he'd done when guiding Debs to the house with the injured dog. Yet the prospect of a meal out with a courteous, pleasant male companion *was* enticing. It was such a long time since she'd been out like that and even longer since she'd felt attractive. She was being foolish. It was only Gilles's way of thanking her for helping Q, as he'd said. Just before Ade had died, she had become too used to reading more into what was said to her and analysing every gesture and look. Since then, well, she was out of practice in listening to men and believing what they said.

The dress she had chosen to wear was blue and gave the impression of being a wrap-around with a tie at the side. A string of blue beads and some matching drop earrings finished the effect. She hoped the colour complemented her eyes and skin tone. As she returned downstairs, Grace was enthusiastic.

"Mum, you look lovely. That colour is just right for you."

"Thank you, darling. I am ridiculously nervous, and it's only a casual outing."

Angela found herself pacing the floor between the window and the mirror in the hall, where she peered at her reflection. Then she sat on the edge of the sofa before rising to pace once more. She was like a jittery teenager. She hurried upstairs to fetch her phone and just then the doorbell rang, making her jump.

Grabbing her bag, she called to Grace, "See you later. Debs will be back any minute."

"She texted me about five minutes ago. She's on her way. Have a nice time. See you."

When Angela opened the door, Gilles stood on the step and smiled at her. He looked smart in chinos and a jacket. His blue shirt, open at the neck, made his skin look very brown. He smelled citrusy and Angela felt a small wobble inside. He looked sheepish and shy, but he took her elbow and guided her down the path, before opening the car door and ensuring she was seated before he closed it for her. Gilles's proximity in the car and the smell of his cologne made her senses tingle. She cleared her throat, trying to dispel her nervous tension.

This might be a disaster, she thought.

When they entered the restaurant, things changed. "It's amazing," Angela said, as she moved swiftly to the glass panel and surveyed the water wheel behind and listened to the water sloshing as it turned. The golden wood panelling inside was warm, and the candles on the tables made the glassware and cutlery sparkle.

"It is a bit different."

After they were seated, the waiter took her thick linen serviette and, with a flourish, spread it across Angela's knees before passing her a huge menu.

"So, my dear Angelique, let us decide what to have to drink first, and then we will talk more easily, I think."

She was grateful to him for sensing her nervousness. There was a cheekiness to his grin, and she laughed. After that, she relaxed, and they began to talk.

Gilles spoke of his late wife, Marie, and her love of all things in the natural environment. Angela was able to refer to her life in London with Ade without the expected onslaught of pain and guilt.

"I'm happier here in a village, though," she said. " Now I look back, I realise that I was there, in London, because of Ade's work. I can work anywhere, though."

"And what is your work, Angelique?" When Gilles used this French form of her name, it felt intimate without being intimidating, and a gentle warmth crept through her.

"I write."

"Yes, of course. You told me before," he said, "but you have not told me of what you write?"

"Novels. For women, mainly, and short stories for magazines. I don't earn a fortune, but enough to mean we can afford a few little extras sometimes. I don't use my own name. So, if you go into a supermarket and see my books on the shelf, you wouldn't know it was me, and neither would the other people in the village. I like that anonymity."

"Wow! I wasn't expecting that. That's amazing. How clever. Will you share with me that information? You know, I *can* be trusted. For you, I wouldn't repeat it to a soul."

She hesitated.

He raised his hands in surrender. "Please, forget I asked. I'm sorry. Truly."

"No, it's all right." She thought for a second. "My writer's name is Christine Ellis."

"But that's nothing like your own name."

She laughed. "I chose my mother's maiden name, and Christine is my grandmother's name."

"Well, that's a coincidence. It is the Christian name of my maternal grandmother also." He raised his glass to her. "Here's to Christine." He sipped his wine, and the candlelight made his eyes twinkle as he gazed at her over the top of his glass.

She cleared her throat and lowered her own gaze.

The rest of the evening passed in a whirl of laughter and chattering. When he dropped her off at Slater's Cottage, it seemed the most natural thing for her to accept his hand as she climbed out of his car. All her angst over how to say goodnight disappeared when he raised her hand and brushed the back with his lips. His eyes met hers, and there was an intensity there that left her breathless.

"Goodnight, my Angelique." And he was gone before she had time to compose herself.

CHAPTER 14

The next morning, Angela gazed out of the window as she stood at the sink. The garden before her blurred as she replayed that kiss on the back of her hand — so innocent but engulfed in passion and unspoken thoughts, certainly on her part. What of Gilles? Was it merely a formal goodnight? Had she really seen that fervency in the look he gave her?

"I've been working on Q," Grace confided to her mum, breaking her train of thought. "I told him he really needs to work hard once term starts and try his best to pass his A-level maths and physics. I'm so pleased Tracey Sutton won't be there next term," she added between mouthfuls of toast.

"Where's she off to?" Debs asked.

"She's left to go to study hairdressing at Stamford College. Milly Paige will be on the bus with me, but that's okay. She won't be in my history class, or my social and cultural class, but she is doing English lit. She's all right, really. I think she'll be better now Tracey's not around."

"This year will be very different, darling," Angela said. "In all sorts of ways. I know you found those last few weeks difficult, but the lower sixth is a different experience. At least you'll know your way around now."

"Mmm. It was probably a good idea to join at the end of last term. I know the teachers. I met Q."

Debs exchanged a glance with Angela, but refrained from saying anything.

They had only a few more days before school began and Angela was pleased Grace and Q wanted to make the most of their freedom. They were going for a bicycle ride that Sunday morning — Grace had steadfastly refused to plead with her mother to buy her a crash helmet so that she could ride pillion on Q's motorcycle, and Angela was relieved. Q had therefore managed to obtain an ordinary bicycle. It had no lights and only one brake, but he and Grace went riding around the countryside back roads as a change from boating.

They often abandoned their bikes once they got as far as the woods and went roaming, on the lookout for deer. Grace was excited when she returned on a couple of occasions. She recounted glimpsing foxes slipping through the undergrowth, and having discovered the den, she was determined to go again in April when there might be cubs.

Angela was sitting at her desk, reminiscing about her own days when at that age. With her, it had been her brother and his friends with whom she had roamed the same woodland. She remembered the loamy smell after rain and the wetness of the leaves and grass brushing her bare legs as they pushed their way through the undergrowth. They had found a badger set and often went back just as the sun was descending.

Towards the end of August, the weather broke. Waterthorpe was lashed by rain and gales, spinning down a few bronzing leaves. When he was not obliged to help his grandfather, Q came to Slater's Cottage and he and Grace did their holiday homework together, played Xbox games, or sat listening to music, talking, and teasing each other. Angela watched with envy. They were wholly content. If they exchanged a few experimental kisses when Angela was not in the room, she pretended to suspect nothing, telling herself it was normal for their age. Debs did not agree and glowered at Q whenever she encountered him. As she was out working much of the time, harmony reigned, and Angela got down to some serious writing at last. On one or two wet evenings, she told Q to telephone his grandfather and invite him to supper. Afterwards, they played Scrabble with considerable bursts of merriment, mostly over Gilles's inability to make good English words, and even Debs relaxed enough to join in once.

As Angela sat at her desk waiting for her laptop to start up, she was feeling crabby — unusual, these days. She stared out of the window, trying to work out why and denying that it was because she hadn't seen Gilles for several days.

I wonder why he declined the last invitation to come here, she thought. *The excuse he gave was feeble. Perhaps he thinks I've been too persistent.*

She was preparing to write when the telephone rang.

"Huh," she sighed. "Now what?" She picked it up. "Hello?"

"Mrs Ross?" The voice was a little hoarse.

"Yes. Who is this, please?"

Several deep breaths sounded in Angela's ear.

"Who is it?" she asked again, preparing to cut the call.

"Er … Alan Cooper. Um … is, is your daughter there?"

"Do you mean Debs or Grace?"

"Er … Debs. The … er … vet. Could she, do you think… My bitch is whelping. Having a spot of trouble."

Before Angela could form any reply, Debs burst into the room.

"Is that for me?"

"Yes. Alan Cooper at Home Farm. Apparently in need of your veterinary skills … again," Angela said in a dry tone, handing over the phone.

"Hello," Debs said. "Ah, yes. All right, Alan. Don't do anything more. I'll be along in five minutes." She flung the phone back into its cradle.

"Doesn't hesitate to call you when he's having a spot of bother, does he? Cheap round for him. Hadn't you better start charging him for making use of your professional services?"

At the door, Debs spun around. "What exactly do you mean?"

Angela was, for once, thoroughly annoyed. "Surely he must have a regular vet? Saving himself expense to call you, I suppose."

"Well, you suppose wrong." Debs flushed scarlet with wrath. "That farm was going to rack and ruin before Alan took it over. Everyone says so. He's built it up to a prosperous business practically single-handed. His usual vet lives in Peterborough, and I don't mind giving a hand to a ... a friend."

"I'm sure you don't, but isn't it becoming a bit of a habit?" Angela knew she was spoiling for a fight, but a worm in her brain made her pursue the line she had taken. "You're at his beck and call."

"I'm not at his beck and call. Oh, I can't stay and argue now. It's that collie bitch's first whelping and Alan's fearing trouble. I promised I'd help when I was there the other day." Debs flounced out, slamming the study door.

Angela sighed, regretting her hasty interference. She was contrite about her criticism, but it was too late to say. It wasn't Debs's fault that she was in such a tizzy about her own developing friendship.

Angela would be so pleased for her daughter if she found a partner. If only Debs realised that and shared her feelings with her mother, just a little. But Angela hadn't helped their relationship with that spat.

It was evening before Debs returned. Angela and Grace had had supper earlier and were watching television. Debs carried a basket of newly laid eggs, which she dumped in Angela's lap.

"Alan sent you those."

"Sent me ... again? He sent some once before. Well, he must have meant these for us all, of course."

"I don't think so," Debs said with a set look on her face. "He said, 'Give these as a present to your mother.'"

"As a thank-you to you, I'm sure, for helping him. How's the dog?"

"Alive, just about. Four pups. First was stillborn and two others quite weak. The fourth seems all right." Debs paused. "Alan said, if you like, he'll send up some eggs every week. No charge."

Angela was astonished. "How very kind, but if it's in lieu of payment to you..."

"It isn't. I told you earlier, I don't expect payment from a friend. It hasn't anything to do with me. They're presents for you."

"He's a kind and generous man, Debs. My outburst this morning was wholly unfair and I'm sorry. I was feeling irritable. I shouldn't have said what I did. It wasn't your fault or Alan's, and I was taking my bad mood out on you both."

"Doesn't matter." Debs shot out of the room, and they heard her thudding upstairs.

"Goodness, Mum," Grace said and laughed. "I do believe you're capturing the hearts of all the men in Waterthorpe. Gilles Richard. Now Alan Cooper. And Q thinks you're the cat's whiskers."

"Does he?" Angela stared at the television without seeing or hearing it properly.

An astounding notion had crossed her mind as she thought about Debs's angry face. Not only angry, but also unhappy. She knew Debs was trying to conceal her feelings as she often did, usually by being feisty. Was it possible? Could Debs be falling for that stiff-necked, awkward, unsociable farmer? And why on earth was the wretched man bent on sending her, Angela, gifts? He couldn't be thinking… But he must be much closer in age to herself than Debs.

Oh Lord! Surely she's not jealous of me? Oh, she must be mistaken. She's an independent, strong-minded young woman of twenty-five, thought Angela. *Could she fall for such an awkward guy? Surely not…* Though Alan Cooper was undoubtedly a generous man. They both had an affinity for animals, and Debs was strong and hardworking. She loved the outdoors, too.

Angela smiled and tutted. What a mess. Was this why Gilles hadn't been in touch? Did he suspect that Alan Cooper had a fancy for her? No, no, no! The whole thing was ridiculous.

The next day, when Angela had a chance to speak with Debs, she asked, "Do you happen to know Alan's age?"

"He's thirty-six."

Angela felt an immediate sense of relief. Nine years her junior.

"Good grief, he looks at least fifty," Grace remarked, glancing up from the notes she was writing. She and Q had decided to record their viewings of some of the local wildlife.

"He does not." Debs was up in arms. "If he does appear a little more than his age, it's because he's had to work so hard building up his farm. Single-handed, I might add."

"Wow, Mum, he could be your toy-boy," Grace chortled, ignoring Angela's warning looks.

Debs glared at her sister. "What a vulgar thing to say. It must be due to all the time you're spending with that French boy." She stalked from the room as Grace leapt up, prepared to do battle.

"For heaven's sake, Grace, can't you be more tactful? I think we're going to need to be careful."

Grace stared. "Mum, you can't be thinking she's got a thing for that lump."

"I think she might have. Do watch it, darling, if we want peace around here. And that's not a pleasant way to describe him, not at all. He's a shy man, but he's kind. And if your sister has a thing for him, then we must see beyond his awkwardness."

Grace groaned. "Imagine having Alan Cooper for a brother-in-law."

"You'd prefer him as a stepfather?" Angela asked, raising her eyebrows and smiling, her head on one side. "You accused him of being my toy-boy just now."

They exchanged looks of mutual exasperation, then laughed.

CHAPTER 15

Gilles decided to walk down the lane to see Alan at Home Farm. He hadn't seen his friend for a while, and lately he'd been so wrapped up in his thoughts of Angelique. He had spent so many hours devising ways of glimpsing her as he went about his business and she hers, that Alan had taken second place. He knew this was not right. Alan would be hurt if he neglected him any longer.

"I'm going to see Alan," he called up to his grandson. "To see if his dog has had those pups yet." There was a muffled response and he guessed that Q was still under the bedclothes, so he let himself out of the house and set off up the lane. As he went, he thought about Angelique and their dinner date at The Watermill. Things had been constrained to begin with, but he thought she'd enjoyed the evening. Her eyes, oh, how they had sparkled in the candlelight. He'd liked her dress too — the colour had suited her. The couple of times he'd seen her since then, he'd enjoyed. The Scrabble had been fun, but he'd given such a silly excuse last time she'd invited him over. *I don't want to be too keen and scare her off*, he thought. *She sees me as a friend, but I want so much more. She's fascinating. I want to protect her, to be with her. Ah, life is so complicated and I'm out of practice in this dating game.*

As he neared the farm he could hear noise coming from the barn, so he headed that way. "Hello? Alan, my friend, are you there?"

"Oh, Gilles. I was rearranging these sacks of pellets. I think a rat must have got to them." He avoided Gilles's gaze and carried on with his task.

Gilles was well aware that Alan found it difficult to communicate, especially with people he didn't know well, but he was also sure that the two of them were well beyond that, so he was a little puzzled by Alan's reticence.

Gilles stood and watched. "Want a hand?"

"No, I'm nearly there."

Had he upset Alan? That didn't seem likely. He hadn't seen him in a while. Perhaps that was the problem. "Has your dog had her pups yet?"

"Yes. It was a difficult whelp. One born dead, two still struggling. I'm having to give them supplementary feeds, but I think they'll be all right. It was an all-night job." He carried on with his task, head down.

"You can always ring me if you need assistance, at any time. I've said this before. It's a hard job here on your own," Gilles said.

"You've been busy elsewhere. I hear you're spending time at Slater's Cottage, and even accompanied Debs on one of her missions." He laughed mirthlessly.

Was this the reason why Alan was so short with him? Had he, too, taken a shine to Angela, his Angelique? Oh no.

"Never too busy to help a friend." Gilles smiled at Alan, trying to mask his surprise. It would be devastating to this sensitive, awkward man if he lost a contest for Angelique's love, but what could he do? He was already well on the way to being in love with her himself. He regarded the other man. "That means you as well. Always happy to help," he repeated.

Alan was much younger than her. Maybe that was what drew him to her. She put him at his ease, made him feel valued. That was her natural way. Gilles took a deep breath to steady himself, but his thoughts slithered on. Perhaps she was attracted by Alan's vulnerability as Gilles was by hers.

Gilles ran his finger around his collar. Anger seeped into his heart, but he recognised it for the venomous viper that it was and he emptied his lungs slowly.

After hanging around for a little longer, he decided discretion was necessary, and he said his goodbyes before adding, "Call, my friend, if you need anything."

"Thanks, yes, bye."

As he headed back to his greenhouses, Gilles bumped into Harry. He seemed so happy married to Annie, with his little daughter completing his family. Still, he'd had his problems in the past, apparently. Perhaps there was still hope for Gilles.

As he walked home, he had plenty to occupy his thoughts. Alan had given Angela the flowers. He'd lent her the cultivator, albeit with his assistance.

He tutted at himself. *Didn't I hear that a basket of eggs had gone to her too? Is that why she was initially reluctant to go with me to The Watermill for dinner? And I persisted. Tu est un imbécile. But I do like her so very much. She is brave and generous. I am young again. I think of her when I'm working, and when I'm cooking dinner for Q and me. Surely Alan is much too young for her.*

Gilles discovered he was devastated at the thought of the two of them together. Should he go all out and fight for her, or should he allow her space and time to make up her own mind? Ah, life was so complicated. This was the first time since his Marie had died that he was interested in someone. He'd kept himself to himself because of all that had happened in France. He didn't want that to affect their life here. It was important for Q to grow up without all that. He thought it had worked, but now, when he was finally experiencing this strong desire again, he had a rival in one of his few good friends.

He stopped walking and leaned on a gate, looking across the fields to the wide, grey sky that matched his new mood. His left foot was up on the bottom bar and as he stood, his head dropped onto his arms and he was motionless for several minutes, his heart heavy with indecision.

On arriving back at the house, Gilles called up to Q. "Are you up yet? It's about time you were." When there was no reply, he became tense and irritated. "For goodness' sake, Q. The day is half over. Don't be so lazy." His breath escaped in a rush, and he struck his thigh with the flat of his hand as he turned. "I'm going to the greenhouses."

As he opened the front door and prepared to storm out, he nearly walked straight into Q. "Oh, there you are."

"You look thunderous. What's the problem? I was looking for you down at the lake. I wondered if you wanted me to cut the grass before it rains again."

"I … I thought you were still in bed." Gilles had the good grace to look at his feet and shrug. "I apologise. It would be very good if you would get out the mower. Here's the key. I know you enjoy driving it, but it would indeed be helpful. Thank you."

"Is there anything else I can do? I was going to see Grace later, but we've nothing definite planned. Only, well, you seem a bit out of sorts. Are you still coming for supper? You haven't forgotten that you are invited, have you?"

"No, I've not forgotten, but I think I must make my apologies. I really need to catch up here with some paperwork. You go, though. Perhaps you would take a note to Angela, when you go later, if I write one. Right, I'll be off. See you soon." With that, he strode away with his head down.

He would have to forego this evening now. After seeing Alan and thinking about it, perhaps it really would be better to give

Angela space to decide what, or who, she wanted in her life. He must keep his own company again. This seemed doubly hard since he had glimpsed a new relationship, experienced attraction like never before and dreamed of close companionship once more after the desert of the last few years.

CHAPTER 16

Since the day that Ranger had knocked Ben over, the rough sleeper's manner changed. He no longer scrambled away to hide when he saw Angela and the dog approaching but stayed in his sheltered corner of the quarry, the autumn sun warming his old body. He even nodded agreement to any comment she made regarding the weather, sometimes smiling his shy, sweet smile. Angela still had some curiosity about him and his origins, but she had grown accustomed to seeing him almost daily and knew that he posed no threat.

The harvest festival at Michaelmas was a great occasion in Waterthorpe. Angela and her two daughters attended the service at the church, sitting with Angela's friend, Pat, and her husband. The spectacle of fruit, vegetables, loaves, and tins was rich with autumnal colours. One of the farmers had donated some sheaves of corn and the 'ladies who do' had clearly spent hours arranging vast branches of umber beech and mottled maple leaves, to complete the display. It was comforting to sing all the old familiar hymns of her childhood, and when the children of the local school sang the more modern 'Cauliflowers Fluffy and Cabbages Green', smiles crept over the faces of the whole congregation as they tapped their feet to the jaunty rhythm.

Gilles was there. She spied his curly black hair and his tall, broad-shouldered frame as soon as she'd entered the building, despite her determination to play this friendship slow and cool. She was aware of his furtive glances in her direction. Although she had smiled and nodded at him on arrival, at the end of the service when most people hung around for a chat and exchange of news, he was nowhere to be seen. Q came over to see Grace.

"Has your *grandpère* gone already?" she asked as innocently as she was able.

"Yes, he said he had some paperwork to do," Q replied and avoided her eyes.

That old excuse, Angela thought.

The next day she helped transport all the fruit, vegetables and loaves that had decorated the altar to the village hall for the annual harvest supper and produce sale. That evening, Grace and Q spent a lot of time bidding against each other for pots of homemade lemon curd but were finally beaten by an outlandish offer in the auction from the vicar, which caused much hilarity. There was no sign of Gilles. Angela's disappointment gripped her heart, but what could she do to put him from her thoughts? His image crept into her mind when she was least expecting it, yet she was the one who had prevaricated about any relationship developing.

Autumn passed swiftly, and winter sprang upon the village in mid-December following a day of thick, dank mist. By the next morning, snow was falling in fat flakes that covered everything with silent speed, and this was succeeded by days of freezing temperatures that ensured the snow stayed put; roofs, fences, tree branches, and garden shrubs were under a layer of hoar-frosted ice. People meeting in the street on their way to Miss Brooks's shop greeted each other with clouds of steamy breath and gloomy forecasts of a bad winter ahead. For two days, until the snow plough arrived, the village was cut off. Free of school, the young amused themselves with snowball fights and a competition to build the best snowman. Q and some others built a gigantic one on the cricket field and then snowballed it down. Angela and Grace went to watch and exercise Ranger there, for the path to the quarry was almost impassable. Angela thought often of Ben and wondered how he could be surviving.

On the third morning, the roads were all open, so the children went reluctantly back to school; the girls were slipping and giggling and the boys, sliding and throwing clods of iced snow at each other. The bridle path was just about useable too. Clad in boots, her thickest coat, and a woollen scarf, Angela struggled through uneven drifts of snow to reach the quarry with Ranger. The dog was not her real reason for making the effort. As she tramped through the coppice, all was silent except for swirls of wind shaking ice-bound branches, causing twigs to clink beneath a pewter sky.

She did not quite know what she was expecting. After all, poor Ben must be used to coping, even with such vile weather as this.

She had consulted Pat about him, but her friend merely shook her head sadly and said, "There's nothing to be done, Angela. Several people tried in the past, but Ben won't accept help. Last winter, Alan Cooper offered him a duffel coat that was almost new. Ben just threw it down in a patch of snow and stamped off."

"But where can he find food?"

"I don't know. I dare say he begs from somewhere. I've seen him near that garage café on the main road. Or, I suppose, he may rifle through dustbins."

"He must have survived bad winters before, but he's older now and he limps badly. Hasn't anyone contacted Social Services about him?"

Pat looked curiously embarrassed. "As a matter of fact, I asked my husband to make enquiries a couple of years ago when we had a particularly bad cold spell, but the person he saw said, as far as they were concerned, Ben doesn't exist. No paperwork and no records, so he's not entitled to any benefits without going in to register. There are dozens of homeless people roaming around, especially in towns. If Ben ever owned a pension book, I expect he lost it years ago."

"Doesn't exist!" Angela repeated, scandalised.

"It does seem awful, but I suppose it's difficult. Modern systems demand records of some sort, some verification," murmured Pat. "Perhaps if Ben himself went to ask for assistance…"

"Small hope of that, I should think. What if he becomes seriously ill?"

"Send for the police, I suppose. But I'm doubtful…"

"I know I'm still comparatively new here," Angela said. "You've all lived with the situation for years. It just seems so awful."

"It is awful, but it's no use worrying about him. We've tried, and either the authorities or Ben himself have prevented anything from happening."

Angela did worry, though. She was intensely compassionate and as temperatures dropped lower and lower, and weather forecasts spoke of it being the coldest spell for decades, she was appalled by the thought of anyone sleeping rough, never mind seeking scraps of food from rubbish bins. In the city, temporary shelters were set up. The parish church, in the centre, opened its doors during the daytime and people served hot drinks. The cathedral allowed the homeless to sit inside, provided they weren't actively begging from visitors. Out here in the country, there was nothing like that. She lay awake at night listening to the silence and wondering how the old man could possibly survive. She got up, desperate to see if more snow had fallen. The sky was scattered with sequin silver stars and the slim curve of a waxing moon caused the same sparkle on the snow below. There had been no further fall but still Angela was distraught at the thought of the old man.

Arriving at the quarry, she saw Ben at once. He had worn a path walking around in a circle, striving for some warmth by flapping his arms across his body looking weary and dispirited. As she passed, she nodded and tried to smile. He gazed at her but did not pause in his slow circling. Was he hungry? Surely, he must be starving. Where in this wasteland could he find anything to eat? Proud he might be, but could a starving man actually refuse food? This certainly put her own problems into perspective.

Angela hurried home. Half an hour later, she was back in the quarry with a packet of thick cheese sandwiches, an apple, and a thermos of warming soup. Ben was still pursuing his hopeless round. Even so, Angela went towards him nervously. From stories elsewhere, she was unsure of the reception her gift would receive.

"Will you take these?"

He did and stood with the sandwich package clutched to his chest, and the flask encircled by his broad, thick-nailed fingers. His gaze fastened on her face, a mix of puzzlement and wonder. As she turned away, she heard him tearing at the wrapping.

"Leave the flask by that rock," she said over her shoulder, pointing. "I'll collect it later."

Angela did not see Ben again for nearly a week, though she visited the quarry every day. Each time she took food in a plastic box and a hot drink in the thermos flask to leave by the boulder and they disappeared, the empty containers left in their place when she returned. She told no-one of what she was doing, except Grace. Not even Debs, whose reactions were so unpredictable. She ensured Grace would not tell Q. The rest of the village were not to know. They would think her soft or worse, irresponsible and meddling — starting something which they might believe would not be maintained.

She had seen little of Gilles in recent weeks and was piqued by the fact, and not a little puzzled. Were they not friends? The other side of her brain, however, told her she didn't mind. Over the years her confidence had waned, having allowed herself to live in Ade's shadow. Her lack of certainty over her relationships with others was often overwhelming.

She knew something of the history of the people at Moondreams House — Natalie, who ran the teashop and who had been abandoned at birth, and Annie, who was now so happily married with the child she didn't think she would ever have. Even David Troughton, the owner of the House, was finding his feet again after years in the wilderness of depression and apathy, apparently.

Having left it too late to confront Ade, Angela knew she should speak to Gilles, but she couldn't. She simply couldn't.

CHAPTER 17

Throughout the early part of the autumn, gifts had kept appearing on Angela's doorstep. Sometimes it was free range eggs. A pitcher of fresh cream arrived one day. Another week there was a chicken, plucked and ready for the oven, all wrapped in tinfoil. They must have come from Alan Cooper, and Angela was torn between gratitude and horror at being beholden to him. Debs, who knew him best, flatly refused to make any sort of protest, so eventually Angela had plucked up the nerve to go to Home Farm and offer payment. Red-faced and obviously distracted, though not offended, the farmer had kept refusing.

"But I want your family to have them. Debs has been so helpful to me. She's become a friend, Mrs Ross. If they're useful…" He trailed off.

"Of course they're useful. It's so kind of you, Alan, but truly…"

"Please, let me." He pleaded so simply that she could not refuse.

Nevertheless, it bothered her, especially when Pat Singleton remarked teasingly that the villagers were laying bets as to who would win her favour, the French captain or the farmer.

"Oh, but that's quite ridiculous," Angela said, indignant and acutely embarrassed. "You make it sound like *Far from the Madding Crowd*. I've hardly seen Gilles Richard and as for Alan Cooper, well… Really, I do wish people would mind their own business."

"Not much chance of that in a village like this. Don't take it to heart, Angela. No one means any harm. Everyone likes you and wants you to be happy."

"I am happy. I'm happy as I am, without seeking anything more." Then, after a pause, she said, "Alan's closer to Debs than to me, anyway."

Her own words were a revelation to her when she thought about them on her way back home. Perhaps that was it. He was trying to impress her daughter.

And now here they were. It was the first Christmas without Ade Ross, so inevitably there was some wistful sadness at Slater's Cottage, but it was now nearly a year since the fatal accident. Angela and her daughters were each in a different place, both physically and emotionally.

There had definitely been tension between her and Ade during his last few weeks, she had come to realise. She'd tried hard to rationalise his distant behaviour. He'd been working extra hours. He'd said it was a rush job that needed his oversight. He'd been tired. He'd been concerned about the business. She'd had so little time between seeing him with the redhead and him dying under the wheels of that van. Did she regret not confronting him? Yes. What would she have done if his infidelity had been confirmed? She didn't know. The girls may never have forgiven her if she'd chucked him out. Would she have forgiven herself if she hadn't? Probably not. Loyalty and trust were her two watchwords. She couldn't decide if it would have been braver to let him stay and try to make the best of it for the children, or cowardly not to face life on her own without him.

Now, this Christmas, for the first time Angela began to realise how she was growing into her new life among her friends. The loneliness was still there, but perhaps she was learning to live with it. She and the girls went next door for a pre-Christmas dinner drink. The Singletons' children and grandchildren were staying for the festive season, so it was a lively session. By the time they sat down for their dinner back at home, Angela and the two girls were ready to enjoy some quiet pleasure.

In response to Grace's pleading, Angela had finally gritted her teeth and invited Q and Gilles Richard for the Boxing Day evening meal. The idea of a friendship was fine, she had decided. Anything more, then no. Seemingly he wanted no more either. She also invited Alan Cooper to eat with them. After all, he was on his own and maybe, just maybe, a gentle shove might help him see what was under his nose in terms of Debs. She thought he was lonely, too. Probably he was trying to make friends with all of them in the only awkward way he knew how. Debs said he had no relatives except a married sister who lived down south and whom he never saw. He was too busy to leave the farm, and she didn't come up this way. Debs, however, had been very offhand when she'd mentioned her intention to invite him. Her older daughter would never admit her feelings.

This could be a tense evening, Angela decided as the time drew close, and she wasn't at all sure she was looking forward to it, since they had all accepted her invitation.

"In the spirit of friendship," Gilles had said.

"A season for friends," Alan had unconsciously echoed.

Alan arrived wearing what was probably his best dark suit, well pressed, and his thick, fair hair was slicked down with gel. When Gilles and Q arrived, they were dressed in casual trousers and pullovers. Angela's prickle of anxiety increased tenfold. They must each have arrived with different expectations.

Gilles, however, carried the conversation with easy charm in his soft, deep voice, until wine loosened all their tongues. Angela was grateful. Debs had come a little late, but her mother noted that she had made the most of her appearance, wearing a dark crimson dress, a gift from herself. The rich colour made her skin glow, and her eyes and hair shone in the candlelight. Alan and she began an amiable conversation about sheep diseases, and as usual, Grace and Q were easy with each other.

They had finished eating and were gathered round the fire when a phone rang. Debs went to find it and came back looking gloomy.

"That was mine. Mum, I'm sorry but I'll have to go out. Peter Carpenter has slipped and broken his right arm and there's an emergency over at a farm near Deeping St James."

"Oh, what a pity. Poor Mr Carpenter. Are you okay to drive? You haven't drunk too much?"

"I only had one, and that was with the meal. I'll be fine. Can't be helped. I'll go and change."

Angela looked hopefully at Alan, wondering if he would offer to accompany her, but he sat in silence.

As Debs left the room, Gilles took the opportunity to stand, too. "I must go, too. I have an early start."

"Oh no, so soon?" Angela frowned.

Grace looked from one adult to another. "It's not late. Q can stay, and we can finish the game we've started, can't we?"

"Yes, of course," Gilles said, turning to Angela. "If that is all right with you." At the door, he raised her hand to his lips, but turned it over and kissed her palm. "*Bon nuit. Mon coeur*," he added in a whisper as he turned away. She was surprised into silence.

The snow had stopped, and the path was lit by bright moonlight. He turned. "*Dors bien.*"

Too late, she thought of all the responses she could have given. Would she sleep tight? She doubted it.

After Debs had gone, Alan said abruptly, "I shall wash up for you, Angela."

"Indeed you won't." She laughed lightly. "It will go in the dishwasher, and Grace will help me to tidy away tomorrow."

"Tomorrow? You can't leave all those dishes till then." He paused. "It can be my thanks for inviting me here this evening."

"Let's leave them till morning," Grace pleaded as she hung onto the doorframe and poked her head round after hearing her name, but Alan had already begun piling the used plates and carried them through to the kitchen. Angela followed him. She was puzzled about why he hadn't taken the opportunity to leave with Gilles.

She had her own method in the kitchen, so she jumped in and said, "I'll load the dishwasher, if you want to make a start on those pans. Just stack them on the draining board and I'll put them away later."

They worked in silence for so long that she began searching for some light topic to relieve her growing disquiet. "I'm sorry Debs had to leave."

"Yes, indeed. She's conscientious. She's been good to me, too." There was another prolonged silence. Then Alan said, "I think your older daughter is a lonely person."

Astonished by his perception but instantly on the defensive, Angela said, "Debs doesn't make friends as easily as Grace. She's more reserved. There's a French girl she worked with, Jeannette Garot. Debs made friends with her when she did a year over there after her finals. She's invited her and her mother, who's a widow, to come over and visit us in the spring."

Apparently, Alan could find no comment but muttered presently, "Debs is good with animals. I think she makes an excellent vet."

Was this why he stayed, so that he could talk about her daughter? He should have gone with her.

"Oh yes, she's very keen on her work and animals react well to her. Ranger loves her."

Hearing his name, the collie looked up from his bed and thumped his tail.

Then Alan blurted out, "You. You too, are kind. It has been a great pleasure to be invited here tonight to be with your family."

Unsure where he was going to go with this, Angela glanced at him, but his flushed cheeks and avoidance of eye contact indicated his embarrassment. He grabbed a cup to rinse in the sink and crashed it against the tap in his agitation. The movement was so forceful that the handle came off. He looked at her in acute distress.

"Please don't worry," she said with haste. "It was an accident. I dare say I can stick it back on."

Alan seemed so ludicrously relieved that Angela felt genuine sorrow for him, which ground away her irritation.

"Come back by the fire and have one last drink before you go?"

Q and Grace had moved next to the fireplace and were lying on the rug with a chessboard between them. Alan looked at them and said, "That's better than computer games. I used to play with my mother." But then he refused her offer. "No. No thanks. It's time I went."

"A cup of tea and a piece of cake?"

"No, thank you. No cake. I'm diabetic. Must take a look at the stock before turning in. Better head off."

Angela fetched his coat and when she opened the front door, an icy blast gushed into the hall. She was grateful that Debs had a reliable car. The wind was strong and drifts of snow from the fields would blow across the tarmac in this.

"Goodnight, Alan. I'm so pleased you were able to come." Angela aimed for a formal tone.

He seized her hand and pumped it up and down. "Thank you. Thank you. You have a lovely family, and it was so generous to invite me. Please wish Debs a goodnight when she finally returns."

He edged outside. Angela stood on the step, rubbing her arms as she watched him walk down the path to the little gate with a sense of relief that she couldn't deny, despite her best intentions. He turned and waved as he disappeared down the road, and she returned to the cosy sitting room.

Did he have a fancy for her older daughter? He was such a tense man, it was impossible to say. She was fairly certain Debs liked him. That surely must be the reason for all the gifts he silently left on her step. Still, there was a hint of uncertainty.

Alan should have grasped the opportunity to accompany Debs, the idiot, Angela thought. As for Gilles, there was a conundrum, indeed. He had shot off at the earliest opportunity, but he'd said those words — *my heart*, and kissed her palm. A spasm deep inside made her shiver. Had he said that, or had she imagined it in her fog of fatigue? She was so utterly weary after the tension of the evening.

But he had kissed her palm. How erotic it had been, now that she replayed the moment. She hadn't imagined that. This was ridiculous. She didn't want any kind of intimate relationship. Now, her palm tingled from his lips. She stared at it before enclosing his kiss inside her furled fingers.

CHAPTER 18

Angela was still tired the next morning. She had slept fitfully, with weird dreams waking her every couple of hours. She decided to go for a walk with Ranger to clear her head. She left a note for Grace, still under the covers. She probably wouldn't emerge before she was back.

As she approached the quarry, Ben emerged from some bushes, limping, but with a little colour in his sunken, roughened cheeks. She saw his hands shaking. What harshness must he have suffered to be afraid of an ordinary woman like herself? He seemed to be overcoming that as he tentatively advanced. She was certainly no longer afraid of him.

"I w-want to thank you, ma'am. Th-thank you."

"You didn't take the socks," she said gently.

"No, ma'am. C-couldn't use 'em. They'd get wet, and I've no way of drying 'em off." His husky voice stuttered, and he looked away.

"You could light a fire. I'll give you matches."

She saw him recoil.

"No, no. Don't like fires." He took a step backwards and his mild eyes were pleading. Pleading for what? Understanding? But all Angela's protective instincts were roused, crushing any need for caution.

"You can't hope to keep warm. Where do you sleep? Do you need more clothing? More food? A blanket? I can easily spare one."

"No, ma'am, really, thanks. I'm not in need of anything now."

"I'm sorry," she gasped. "Oh, I'm sorry." What right had she? "It's just this bitter, dreadful weather."

He smiled then, that gentle smile. "You're kind … but I can't carry extra stuff around, see, and I daren't leave it back where I sleep. It might get stolen, or the twiggy might get it."

"The twiggy?"

"Little animal. Like a weasel. I call him the twiggy. Put anything down and he's on it, quick as a flash." His two fists punched the air in front of him.

Angela didn't know what to make of that, so she said, "You'll let me carry on bringing you food and hot drinks?"

"I'd be obliged, if it's no trouble?"

"No trouble. I come here each day with my dog, as you know."

"Yes, I've seen you." Even in those few minutes of speech, his voice had become stronger. He looked at her under shaggy brows. "Before your sandwiches, I'd had nothing for days, but I'd found some cabbage leaves off the dump."

Angela could hardly suppress a shudder.

"It's amazing," Ben said. "Truly amazing."

"What's amazing?"

"You, bringing me these lovely sandwiches. Even that Christmas card with a cheeky robin on it. Didn't know it was Christmas."

After a moment, she asked, "How long have you been on the road?"

He shrank away a little. "A long time. Over thirty years, maybe. I have to go now. Things to do. It's amazing, absolutely amazing." He was already turning away.

She watched him stumble towards the woods before continuing her walk with the dog. Things to do? Obviously not. He'd had enough, and she was enquiring too closely.

The snow and ice on which she trod crunched, and she slipped and slid on it, not going far before she turned around and called Ranger to her. The dog came bounding along with a hop and a skip, pleased to be out in any weather.

By the time she got home, Angela was in a better frame of mind. Q had returned, and he and Grace were in the kitchen, getting themselves something to eat.

"Did you sleep all right?" Angela asked them both.

"Mm," came a mumbled response from Grace as she sat with a mouth full of cereal.

"Thank you, yes," Q answered.

He might be a bit wild sometimes, but he's a nice lad. Simply a teenager, Angela thought.

When they were on their own again, Grace said, "Why on earth didn't Alan go with Debs last night? If he fancies her, he should have jumped at the opportunity. Really, he is a div."

"Grace don't be unkind, and that's not a very nice expression either," Angela remonstrated. "I'm sure it's complicated. He's very shy and doesn't want to push himself. You know what Debs is like. She can be forthright. Perhaps he's frightened of rejection."

"All these gifts he brings — he doesn't fancy you, does he?"

"No. That's definite," Angela said.

"I don't mind if you find someone else. I know you're, well, older. You know. But if you find someone else now Dad's gone ... I mean..."

"I know what you mean. Come here." Angela stretched out her arms and enfolded Grace, smiling to herself. Older? Yes, but she didn't feel it. It had been an awkward sentiment for her child to utter. "I have no intentions at the moment. I'm quite happy with just the two of us."

"Actually, that's good," Grace said. "I thought I'd better say it, but I prefer it like this, just the two of us, and Debs, of course, when she's here."

All through January and into early February, winter continued to grip the country. No more snow fell, but temperatures were some of the coldest since records began in the middle of the 1600s. Each morning, Angela took food to the quarry. Often, she didn't see Ben for three or four days at a time, and worried accordingly, but the thermos always emptied, and sandwiches disappeared, so she concluded he was managing to survive. Q mentioned he had heard that the old man lived in a broken-down railway hut on a disused local line about half a mile from the quarry.

The shivering light shone through the skeletal branches as Angela took her daily stroll. This time, Ben approached with his head down, his long, matted hair tucked around his neck like a scarf, and there was frost in his beard. He stood without a word until Angela was prompted to ask, "What is it, Ben?"

"I don't like to ask." He paused. "Have you any old newspapers, ma'am?"

She knew the homeless people in the city wrapped themselves in papers and cardboard for warmth, but could not resist offering Ade's old sleeping bag, only to have it politely but firmly refused. "Thanks, ma'am, but I couldn't carry it round with me, could I?"

It would be useless to argue, so she ordered newspapers from Miss Brooks's shop. "Although I won't read them," she told Grace. "Television news is depressing enough."

In two evenings, Angela knitted Ben a pair of gloves from thick navy wool and was still finishing them when Debs came home early and asked for whom they were intended. Angela, with her head down, told her they were for the occupant of the quarry, adding that she had been giving him food and hot drinks for nearly a month. Debs stared for a moment before she astonished Angela by flinging her arms around her, almost knocking the knitting needles out of her hands.

"Mum, that's marvellous, simply fantastic. You really are so kind and good."

Praise from her older daughter was rare and momentarily rendered Angela speechless with pleasure.

"It's only what anyone would do," she said, bending her head to see to a dropped stitch but managing to blink back her tears.

"Ah, but they haven't, have they? It's one thing to talk with sympathy about a man in Ben's position, another to actually do something practical."

"He was starving. I mean really starving. For days he'd had nothing but rotting cabbage leaves off a rubbish dump. He told me."

"Ew! Makes you want to throw up, doesn't it?" Grace said.

"Mum, something should be done about that poor guy," Debs added.

"Easy to say that, Debs. Pat Singleton told me she and her husband made enquiries, but folk like Ben, well … they don't exist officially."

"But they do exist," Debs exploded. "Someone actually starving in England in this day and age. It's ridiculous!"

"I know, but there are dozens like Ben in the cities. They're exposed to drugs and alcohol. Others prey on their weakness."

"People in the city help the homeless. There are at least some facilities. Out here in the countryside, it's far worse and Ben isn't an addict, according to what you're saying."

"Not now, anyway. How could he be? He's isolated out here. He's no money. He's totally destitute. And I dare say," Angela added, "he wouldn't even be able to face living with people around him again, now. He couldn't live what we call a normal life. He told me he's been 'on the road' for more than thirty years."

Debs looked thoughtful. "I've never even seen him. Mum, now you've made this breakthrough, you must try and find out more about him."

"If I can. In time. He's like a forest creature, though; he's timid, afraid of people. I can see he doesn't like me questioning him."

"I suppose you've told Pat, next door, that you're feeding him. What does she say?"

"I haven't told her. I haven't told anyone. I thought, well, they might think I'm interfering. After all, we're comparative newcomers. They might think it's a kind of criticism of them that I'm doing it."

"Hm, you've told Grace, though, I'm sure." There was a bitter edge to Debs's voice.

"Only because she found me making sandwiches." Angela tried to sound apologetic. "I've forbidden her to tell even Q."

"Well, I think the locals ought to know what you're doing."

"No, Debs, please," Angela said with alarm. "I'd much rather people didn't know. It's nothing really. Only a few sandwiches."

"And cake, and soup or tea, sausages, biscuits, fruit, the lot, I bet. I know you, Mum. No half measures. You can't afford it on your income."

"I can and I must. The writing helps. I just do a bit extra when I'm cooking for us."

"Then you must let me help financially. I'm earning now. I shan't take no for an answer."

Angela protested no more. As she put down her knitting and opened her arms to her daughter, she hoped Debs recognised that her profuse thanks were for more than an offer of financial help.

As the days passed, Angela began learning a little more about the man of the woods. Ben's moods were variable. Often, he did no more than thank her, always that, for the food and drink. Now and then, he appeared eager to talk.

"I've been just about everywhere," he volunteered one morning. "Land's End to John O'Groats." There was a ring of pride in his voice. "Till my feet got bad. Came back here, then, to settle."

"Came back? You used to live here?" Angela asked with caution.

He nodded. "Born the other side of Waterthorpe. We moved north when I was six months old, so my father told me. He worked the barges."

"Barges?"

"Manchester Ship Canal."

"Did you have a job?" Angela was keen to know more while he was in voluble mode.

"Used to work on a farm. Then I mowed grass for the council. Not here. Up Chester way. After the war."

"World War Two? Were you a soldier?" Surely he wasn't that old.

"I was. No, the Troubles. Ireland."

She saw his expression change. It was subtle, but his mild hazel eyes clouded. "That was bad. T-t-terrible. I don't want to think about that. I can't."

Angela was shaken by the sudden agony in his voice. But now she was even more curious, longing to know more about him, to understand. "After the Troubles, did you become ill?"

"Yes, ill. I was ill." He looked vague. "Couldn't hold a job, so I started walking. Till my feet got bad. Couldn't live under a roof now. I've known some rotten winters, though."

Angela ventured, "Couldn't your family have helped?"

He looked away. "We fell out. Mother died when I was twelve. Lived with me brother for a bit. He got divorced and remarried. That woman! The one my brother married. Awful. Got to go now. Things to do. But thanks." He waved the gloves over his shoulder.

"Take care. Don't lose them." She laughed gently.

He stopped and turned. "No, mustn't lose 'em. Mustn't put 'em down or the twiggy might get 'em."

As he trudged away, the rustling of the plastic around his feet stayed with Angela.

On another occasion, he opened a conversation by remarking, "Still bitter, isn't it?" But I'm all right. I can look after m'self. It's just this damned cold weather. All the refrigerators."

"Refrigerators?" Angela was mystified.

"Folk opening them all the time. Makes for all this ice, I reckon. People should keep those doors shut in winter time."

He gazed at her solemnly and she didn't know how to answer. Perhaps this was what Pat Singleton had meant when she'd said, "Poor Ben, he is a bit touched, you know."

Angela took a deep breath. "What do you do all day? Besides trying to keep warm, of course? Isn't it dull?"

He gave her a pitying look. "Not dull. Oh no, it's never *dull*. The woods are another kingdom, all quiet and calm and empty except for nature. I watch the birds and squirrels. Busy little things, birds. Then there's the twiggy. Got to keep my eye on him or there'll be trouble. And I do my digitaries."

"What are those?"

"Numbers on the telegraph poles. Something odd there. They won't work out." He sighed. "Be easier if I could write 'em down." He frowned.

Some sort of game he plays to keep himself occupied, Angela thought, and then asked tentatively, "You do read and write, then?"

"O' course." He nodded, but without any rancour at all. "Mind you, I always was a bit of a duffer at school, but I like to read, given the chance. And I like poems."

"I like to write. I write poems and stories."

"Stories are good. You can be anywhere with stories," Ben said.

So, she brought him an exercise book and pencils, and left them for him with the food. She added a couple of *Digest* magazines, too.

The next morning, she found a note with the empty thermos. It was spelled incorrectly but read: *receved with apreaciated many thanks.*

Of course, she had another thing to occupy her mind during those icy winter months, too. She was unsure whether to take any steps towards furthering her friendship with Gilles. She must start forgiving herself for being alive, and for not discovering more about Ade's activities before he'd died. Whatever had happened was over. She had to let it go.

CHAPTER 19

As Gilles walked, his thoughts raged. The Boxing Day meal had held such promise, yet when he'd arrived with Q, there was Alan. That had been an unwelcome surprise if he was honest.

As he trudged home from a rare visit to the local pub, there was time to consider his reaction to his friend's presence. This was jealousy, pure and simple. On the night, he'd covered it by being charming and chatty. He was ashamed of his emotions. He'd come to this village to escape and relinquish close friendships. He had the boy to look after and protect. Is that why he'd left early, allowing Alan to be alone with Angela?

His thoughts about Angela overtook those concerning his friend and neighbour. She'd looked so good in that dress and when she'd laughed, her whole face had lit up. The way her eyes had darted from one guest to another was telling. She'd been anxious to ensure everyone had what they wanted and had leapt up very five minutes to fetch something or to move around the table, pouring and passing. Her generosity was all-encompassing.

He'd managed to keep away for the last few weeks and tried to put her from his mind, but she crept into his thoughts at the most unexpected moments — when he was making an omelette for Q, putting the sheets in the washing machine, polishing the furniture. Then he wondered about her husband, Ade. Adrian? He must have shortened it to sound more on-trend. A bit fancy. He knew he was being over-critical. He didn't even know the man. Gilles decided he could never be voguish like that. *I am what I am*, he thought. If his shirt came untucked, so be it. If his hair was too long and a mess, that was him. He was happy to compromise on many things, but he had to be who he was. Otherwise, any relationship would not last. If Angela preferred Alan, he, Gilles, must live with that — somehow.

He continued down the lane from the pub, until he was beside the farm. He glowered at it but was surprised to see the light high on the end wall of the house, shedding a glow across the yard. There was a glimmer seeping around the barn door, too. At this hour? Gilles knew that Alan checked the animals last thing, but he should have been in his bed by now, or at least in front of the television.

He stopped and stared for a moment, trying to decide whether to go and investigate. Putting aside his angst, he finally entered the gate. He had on his good shoes, so he gingerly slithered across the icy yard and opened the side door to the barn. As he peered around, at first his eyes could discern very little. The single light was high up among the dusty girders and was poor. There was the shuffle and stamping of hooves and the occasional snort, but no human sound.

"Hello? Alan, *mon ami*, are you there?" He listened, before calling again. There was no response and so he turned to leave.

Perhaps Alan had simply forgotten to turn the lights off, although that would be highly unusual.

He walked across to the house and peered in at the windows. There was no sign of life in there. He shrugged. He must have taken himself off to bed and left the lights on. Gilles turned for home, but then he heard something. He stood still. There it was again. He headed back towards the barn.

"Hello?" he called again, but hearing nothing he went further in. And there Alan was, lying on the ground near the cow pens.

"I'm tired. Think I'll just stay here for the night. Wake me in the morning, old friend." He laughed, but it was eerie and unnatural. "Been lifting the hay into the cows." He waved his arm in a drunken fashion.

"God, Alan, are you having a hypo? Where are your door keys?"

"I'm fine. I'll just stay here." He giggled again. "Feeling a bit feeble, got the shakes."

Gilles dug in Alan's pocket. Nothing. Tried another. There they were. He grabbed the keys and ran for the house.

"Oh, come on," he muttered as he dropped the keys while fumbling with the lock in the dark. "*Calme-toi*," he said to himself and took a deep breath. Alan was still conscious. A sugary drink. Maybe he had glucose tablets. Sugar would do. Kitchen first.

Gilles ran along the hallway and shoved open the door. He hardly noticed it ricocheting back off the dresser behind it as he groped for a light switch. His eyes grazed the surfaces and found a packet of sugar alongside a jar of coffee. A spoon was sticking out of the packet. *He doesn't take sugar in his coffee, not as a diabetic*, thought Gilles. *Someone must have been here.*

Panic began to take hold. *Stop. Don't be hysterical. Remember, calm. Under the stairs. Cans of cola. Diet, sugar-free. No good. A red glow… Thank the Lord. One can of regular cola. Perfect. Back out into the hall.*

With the sugar bag in one hand and the can in the other, Gilles rushed back outside and across to the barn.

Reaching Alan, who was still slumped against a bale, he held his friend's head back and poured some of the cola into his mouth, followed by a clod of sugar.

Ignoring the dust and muck on the floor, he knelt in his good trousers and wrapped his arm around his friend, supporting him while he swallowed.

"Stay awake, *mon ami*," he said. "We may be rivals in love, but I don't want to win this way."

"What? What are…"

"Shh. Have another drink."

Alan took the can. Already he was coming around. Gilles was surprised and relieved at the speed of his recovery. His friend sat up and looked around him with a puzzled frown. "I haven't done this for years. I'm so sorry, but extremely grateful. It could have been life-threatening. What can I say? You are such a good friend, Gilles."

"Feeling better? Let's see if you can stand, and we'll get you indoors. You can test your blood and have something more to eat if you need," Gilles said. "Did you have a good meal tonight? Did you take too much insulin? How come you had a hypo?"

"Sorry," Alan said. "Glad you came by, though. I was lifting bales. I started to feel shaky and hot, but I didn't stop in time. Was so busy thinking about Debs. I should've offered to go with her last night. Stupid, I am."

"Never mind that now. You stayed with Angela."

They staggered together across the yard and back into the house. Gilles watched while Alan screwed a new needle into the mechanism for gathering a drop of blood and loaded a test strip into the meter. After the test, he announced, "Okay, it's up to 3.4. I'd better have some cereal, maybe a jam sandwich. I'll be fine now. I'll eat those and test again in half an hour. Thank you, Gilles."

"I'll say goodnight, then. Ring me if you need anything else."

"I will. Thank you again." He extended his right hand and Gilles took it. "By the way, what did you mean when you said something about rivals? I can't remember. Didn't take it in, whatever it was. I wasn't quite with it."

"Oh, nothing, my friend. Goodnight."

As Gilles arrived home, he sighed. He was confused by his ties of friendship and loyalty; his need for love; and by Angela's feelings about her deceased husband and Alan.

Then he remembered yet again. There were all the circumstances of his being here in this English village. He'd managed to bury it over the years. No one here ever mentioned it or tried to find out any more. Perhaps it was wrong of him to want her. He would have to tell her, and that would drive her away anyway. How could she want him, knowing about his past?

CHAPTER 20

Angela hadn't expected any repercussions from the impulse of kindness that had made her invite Alan Cooper for the Boxing Day meal. She met him once or twice in the village soon afterwards, and once he even stopped the tractor he was driving and stepped down to wish her a good morning, before asking after her health and that of her girls.

"It must be difficult for Debs to work in this weather," he said obliquely.

"Er, yes. And for you," Angela replied.

Then, one morning she opened the front door to find a plump goose, plucked and stuffed and wrapped in foil, sitting on the step. She bore it into the kitchen and dumped it on the table, saying to Grace, who was eating breakfast, "For pity's sake, look! It's started all over again. What on earth am I going to do now?"

Debs was away working all that week and staying over at Peter Carpenter's house, who had gone to see his brother for a few days. She had been home for a couple of nights in the new year when a locum had arrived at the veterinary practice, but she was still working much longer hours than usual.

Grace looked up at her mother and said with a grin on her face, "Cook it, and we'll eat it and be thankful we have a follower who brings us such unusual presents."

"Grace don't be daft." Angela could only summon a faint smile for her daughter's teasing. "You know we can't go back to accepting gifts from Alan or anyone else. If he has a fancy for Debs, he should tell her."

"Perhaps it's not Debs," Grace laughed. "Perhaps it's you."

"Don't be ridiculous. We've been through that. It's definitely not me."

"Mum, lots of couples have a huge age gap nowadays."

"Thanks very much. It's absurd. Don't even go there."

"Sometimes it doesn't seem long at all since Dad's accident. Other times, it feels like ages and ages." Grace began fiddling with a spoon and avoided Angela's gaze.

"I know, darling. That's how I feel." Angela paused. "I'd never do anything you don't want me to, Grace."

"Do you want to get married again?"

"Honestly, I don't know. I suppose I have thought about it once or twice. Only in the abstract, I mean, but I'm only forty-five. Half of my life to live yet, and once you go off to college or somewhere… There's no one in mind, though, and there are a lot of steps before marriage. I'd need to find a man who'd have me." She chuckled to try and relieve the tension of the discussion and shrugged her shoulders.

"I suppose if it were anyone, it would be Gilles."

Angela half-laughed again. "Oh, Grace, really. I wouldn't even know if he's interested. There's no suggestion," she said resolutely.

"I bet he is interested. I'm sure he likes you. Q thinks so too."

"Oh?" Angela was not too pleased at the thought of being discussed.

Grace shifted in her chair. "He is nice, but quite old."

"He's sixty-one. Not that old. You said I was old the other day, remember? So, would you mind? I know when we spoke before, you said you prefer it being just the two of us."

Grace looked away, flushing. "Would you want to marry him?" she countered in a muffled tone.

"I like him a lot, but we're a very long way from that. I'm not even considering it. We're friends, that's all," Angela said.

"If you did marry him, we'd have to leave Slater's and go and live at the Gatehouse, I suppose."

"You wouldn't like that?"

Grace shook her head, face still averted.

"It's Q, isn't it?" Angela asked quietly, and her eyes narrowed.

Grace nodded.

"You'd see more, not less of each other."

"He'd be my stepbrother," Grace burst out, "and he's not. I mean, we don't feel like that. He's my boyfriend."

After a moment, Angela said, "Well, don't worry about it. Let's stop talking about marriage. It's not even an option. Plenty of time for making decisions. Like I say, there's no suggestion I will go down that route. Not with anyone, let alone Gilles, so this is all academic. And I promise, I won't do anything you don't like." In a different tone, she went on, "Grace, don't let yourself become too attached to Q. In eight months from now, if he passes his exams, he'll be going away to college. If not, then he may go somewhere to work. Not much for a young man to do around here. He may even … find another girl."

She watched Grace's expression change, shutting her out. Then with quiet dignity, she said, "Q and I don't think we'll ever find anyone else."

Angela opened her lips to argue, to point out that Grace was only sixteen and that Q would have his eighteenth birthday soon. But something in the girl's face stopped her. She'd be wasting her breath. Already it was too late. Soon her beloved child might be badly hurt. Perhaps Debs had been right, and she should have discouraged Q and Grace from seeing so much of each other. However, instinct told her that opposition might only have forced them even closer together and caused her to lose Grace's confidence. Oh, it was hard being a single parent.

"Just bear in mind what I've said, darling. Think about it, please. I don't want you to be unhappy."

"Q won't ever make me unhappy."

Angela closed her lips and then said in a brisker tone, "Now, can you tell me what I'm to do about this?" She pointed to the goose.

"Mum, I think you've got a problem," Grace laughed.

"I know I have. Well, it's my problem. You'd better get going or you'll miss the school bus."

After Grace had gone, she sat for a long while, thinking. She realised Q was becoming more popular in Waterthorpe. Months ago, Gilles had said he thought Grace would be a good influence on the lad, and now Angela thought it might be so.

In recent months, the boy had matured. The village elders no longer shook their heads over him. Q was only too keen to share his Christmas school report, and he told her he was working hard. He'd done passably well in his AS levels. There were signs of developing ambition, and his mock exams for his A levels were more promising. He had a mechanical mind and was never happier than when working with car and boat engines. Angela knew Gilles was hoping his grandson would study for an engineering degree at university, although other avenues might be open to him.

Now, when Q and Grace walked up the village street, her head just reaching his shoulder, his arm lightly around her waist, there were tolerant, kindly smiles. The youngsters had weathered teasing by their peers, so at ease were they in each other's company. Even Debs admitted that Q had steadied and always took good care of her sister.

Grace and Q often did their homework sitting together at the kitchen table at Slater's Cottage, their dark-haired heads close as they wrote. Angela felt guilty knowing that the boy spent so much time at her house, leaving Gilles alone on so many dark, cold evenings, and so she had sometimes invited him to supper. Once or twice, he had come.

On one occasion, their hands had met around the glass of wine Angela had passed him. Her heart gave a jolt and when she raised her eyes to his, he was gazing at her. She managed to stave off any more awkward moments by using a brisk, friendly manner when they were alone.

Another time he'd arrived with sleeves rolled up and wearing a tie that was loosely knotted. He looked devastatingly handsome as he flashed a smile in greeting. Her heartrate spiked, robbing her of breath.

"Good evening, Angelique."

She took the jacket that he held casually over his shoulder, and again their hands brushed. "W-what can I get you to drink?" she asked as he followed her down the passageway. Aware his eyes were following the swing of her hips, her voice was as calm as she could make it.

After supper, Grace and Q left the room and Angela followed their departure with troubled eyes. Left alone, Gilles's hand took hers, lacing their fingers together. "Thank you for such a special evening." His voice was deep and gentle.

His skin was smooth and his long fingers warm and comforting, making her heart race again.

"It was nothing special," she said and took a sip of the cool Sauvignon to give herself time to calm. Then she added, "I wanted to say thank you to you. You're helping me to see my own worth." She hung her head. "I've spent a long time in the shadow of others, trying to be what everyone else needs. Hostess, supporter, mother. It's such a cliché, but it's true."

He said nothing to her confession but raised her hand to his lips before letting her go. She left the table and began to shuffle plates and cutlery about near the sink.

Gilles didn't seem to resent Q spending so much time at Slater's, and often consulted Angela about his grandson's welfare.

"I think he's working harder. Do you think I should go up to the school to check whether they agree?"

"He's desperate to drive a car. Should this be a reward for his better attitude, or is it a right to which he should have access?"

"It's so hard being a parent. All the time I'm analysing what I do and say."

As winter progressed and mid-February at last brought milder weather, Angela began to wonder if she had been mistaken with regard to Gilles's feelings for her. Her feelings for him were strengthening, but she was wary. And then there was Grace to consider. Perhaps Gilles was being kind and simply welcomed her advice as a mother and friend.

Angela tried to solve the problem of Alan Cooper by sending Debs to his house with a note and the goose to tell him that she could not possibly accept gifts. No more arrived, and he ceased to waylay her in the village. Once again, she was both relieved and guilty. She didn't want to hurt his feelings, but she wanted him to make some sort of declaration to Debs, who she was sure was harbouring a deep attraction to him. No way could she ask her prickly daughter about what had happened on the day of the goose's return, but it was some time before Debs came home.

As the months wore on, Angela wondered about Gilles more and more. Before she realised it, she looked forward to his visits and was empty when he left, but no more did he kiss her palm, or say "*mon coeur*".

CHAPTER 21

One cool February morning, Angela walked to the shop to collect a loaf of bread and to get some money from the machine there. She'd had several articles and short stories accepted over the winter, and some were already in print. She had even begun toying with the idea of attempting another novel. Her agent had been so patient, but it wouldn't last. She must produce something worthwhile soon. *Write about what you know* had always been a wise maxim for would-be authors, and she was wondering about developing a youngish widow's journey to contentment. She was not yet sure if she was sufficiently detached from her recent experiences, but the urge to put her ideas on paper slowly started to crystallise.

She was so absorbed that she failed to notice Miss Brooks's expression as the postmistress took the coins Angela held out. It was only when the sour lady remarked, "I hear you've been giving things to that fellow up in the stone quarry," that she became aware of grey eyes staring at her angrily over the counter.

Caught off guard, Angela said, "Oh, who's been telling you that?" *Not Grace*, she thought. *She always keeps her promises.* Debs was strong-willed enough to disregard her mother's wishes, but she too had agreed to keep Angela's daily pilgrimage a secret.

"You've been seen," Miss Brooks snapped darkly. "There's been sheep straying up there. Dan Smith went up to get them back."

Angela pulled herself together. "I've been taking Ben some food and a hot drink each day while the weather's been so bad. He was starving, literally starving. His feet are too sore to allow him to walk far in search of food."

"I can't imagine why you bother buying food for a no-good like him. Wasting your money like that."

Angela was suddenly so furious she forgot caution. "It's my money, so I suppose I may spend it how I choose. Ben might easily have died from hypothermia," she said crisply.

"A dirty old thing like him. He's not worth it."

"That," said Angela, "is a matter of opinion. Despite everything, Ben is still one of Nature's gentlemen."

All at once Miss Brooks's cheeks suffused with colour. "You're daft," she screeched. "I think you're daft. A no-good like him. Been telling you tales, I suppose. Telling you stories about himself. Well, you don't want to believe all the things Benjamin Cooper tells you." Whirling round, she rushed into the room at the back of the shop, slamming the door.

Angela stood staring after her, thunderstruck. Her limbs were quivering as she left the shop and walked back to her cottage. As she went, her mind was racing. Such an unpleasant scene with the postmistress. Then surprise engulfed her. Cooper! Could Ben be related to Alan Cooper? It seemed possible, for she knew that most villages were close-knit and relationships often multiply. Ben was of an older generation than Alan, but he had told her that he had been born near Waterthorpe, so perhaps he and Alan might be cousins of a sort. During the weeks she had been ministering to the old man, she had begun to feel protective towards him. There was never anything other than gentle politeness in his approaches. She found that her wish to know more about him had increased. The obvious person to question was Pat Singleton.

Angela had suspected for some time that Pat knew more than she had divulged, but she still shrank from seeming vulgarly inquisitive. However, Miss Brooks now knew she was giving Ben daily food, so it seemed probable that the entire village would be discussing the matter within days. It was time she admitted what she was doing, at least to Pat. The chance arose the next afternoon, when her friend came around to Slater's Cottage for a cup of tea and they sat toasting their feet by the fire. They had only been seated for a few minutes when Pat remarked, "I've been hearing things about you."

"That I've been feeding Ben in the quarry during winter, I suppose, and giving him warmer clothing."

"You could have told me," Pat said with reproach in her voice.

"I very nearly did once or twice. I'm sorry. I didn't tell anyone except Debs and Grace. I thought, well, I suppose I thought people might think I was interfering."

"Interfering? I told you some folk have been trying to help Ben for years, on and off, but he wouldn't let them."

"Exactly. People would think I was an incomer meddling and thinking myself better than them; that I could do what they had been unable to manage."

"How *did* you manage it?"

"He was just so hungry. Desperate with hunger and cold. And perhaps because I'm a stranger, not local. I don't know much about him." Angela looked at her friend. "I would like to know more, Pat."

"I have thought of telling you. I know you'll understand. But I suppose I felt it might be disloyal."

"Disloyal?"

"I told you we're a bit like a large family here and Ben's one of us, or he used to be. It's a sad tale and I suppose many of us feel a bit guilty about him, even though we've tried."

"Miss Brooks doesn't," Angela stated with unusual venom. "I had an awful scene with her in the post office yesterday. Fortunately, no one else was there to hear. She told me off in no uncertain terms for trying to help Ben."

"I suppose I'd better start at the beginning," Pat said, taking a sip of tea. "I've known Ben for oh, years and years. Since I was about twelve years old, anyhow."

"He told me he was born in Waterthorpe, but he said his family left the district when he was a baby."

"Yes, they did, I believe, but then he came back here when he was about fourteen or fifteen. He and his brother came to live at Home Farm and worked for their uncle as farmhands."

"Uncle?"

"The brother of Alan's grandfather. Alan's father, Joe Cooper, Ben's older brother, was to inherit eventually, when the old man and the grandfather both died. Alan wasn't born until much later, of course. Joe inherited Home Farm and got married. He then divorced and later remarried. It was around that time that Ben Cooper finally left Waterthorpe to go wandering."

"He told me he was ill after being in the army. Couldn't hold down a job."

"It was his time in Ireland that ruined him." Pat nodded. "Before that, he was all right. Always a very nervous lad, I remember. Really highly strung. Good-looking, in a delicate sort of way; fair hair, nice eyes. He was always shy and polite. Everyone in the village liked him back then. Some of the girls thought him handsome when he first came back here. Mary Brooks did. She was crazy about him."

"Miss Brooks?" Angela's eyes widened. "Miss Brooks in the shop?"

"Oh yes. We were a year or two younger than Ben. I told you Mary's father lost his money and she had to go out to work, didn't I? She worked at the GPO in Peterborough and hated it. We were friends, after a fashion. She used to confide in me, though between us, I didn't really care for her much. She was spoilt and made so much fuss when she couldn't have what she wanted. We were kind of flung together, being the same age and having no other girls around at the time."

"And she wanted Ben Cooper?"

"My word, yes. The whole village knew about it."

"I'm surprised, if she was so uppity, that she would look at someone from his background. What did he feel? Was he keen on her?"

"I think he was. She said he was. I think she wanted him because others did, too, and she needed to prove to herself that she could get what she wanted. Mind you, I don't think she understood him either. She was, well, always rather insensitive. Quite pretty, though, I suppose. She was always a tough baby under her polite airs," Pat finished humorously, making Angela smile.

"So, what happened?"

"She professed to be really mad about Ben. He used to write her poems. She showed me one once and made me read it. I didn't really want to do that. It seemed like prying. Mary was actually laughing about it, which was a bit cruel, but she was flattered." Pat frowned. "In a way, though, I think she rather despised him for it. She used to call him 'a great big softie' right to his face. Of course, her parents were dead against Ben. They might have come down in the world, but a mere farmhand, as they saw it, wasn't good enough for their daughter. Mary defied them. She never took notice of anyone if she wanted something. Then he joined the army for some inexplicable reason. Maybe he was worried about his prospects, especially if he wanted to get married. Eventually, after some initial training in Aldershot, down in Hampshire, he got sent away somewhere, not sure where exactly. Goodness only knows what happened. He was hospitalised for a couple of months."

"Was he wounded, then?"

"No, they said it was nervous trouble. He came home on leave, but he didn't seem so very different, not to us, anyway. He was always highly strung, like I said." Pat gazed into the fire. "I remember thinking he seemed a bit preoccupied, but Mary couldn't see any difference. She flung her arms around him and vowed they'd announce their engagement when he came home next time, whatever her parents said. She was only about nineteen, then."

"And did they?"

Pat shook her head. "Ben didn't come home. Mary nearly went wild. Then she had a short letter, which she insisted I read." Pat shook her head. "He said he was posted abroad again. He said she'd better forget him, because he probably wouldn't come back, ever. I did feel quite sorry for her then. She wept and howled and wrote letters to Ben's unit but never got any proper answers. Mary didn't believe in the stiff upper lip. He had gone, and no-one heard anything more for about two years. Eventually, Joe Cooper, his brother, received an official letter to say he had been injured in a bomb attack on a bus that was transporting soldiers back to the barracks in Northern Ireland. There were several deaths, and all the others were injured. It was a huge story at the time. Ben was in hospital for physical injuries but then for longer with continuing mental issues. When he finally came home he was changed, withdrawn. He drank a lot too. In the pub at all hours and often seen on the street, staggering about. People were sorry for him and tried to help, but nothing worked. Presumably, he didn't seek further help."

"And what about Miss Brooks?" Angela was hesitant now. "How did she take it all?"

"She'd changed too. Her father had died. Mary and her mother sold the house and started the shop here. Eventually, Mary was made postmistress and she's been doing it ever since, even though she's due for retirement."

"But Ben, how did she behave towards him?"

"Somewhere along the line, she stopped loving him. Perhaps she was let down when he couldn't make the final commitment to her. Then she really despised him. She thought him feeble and couldn't see that he had been ill. She used to say to me, 'He's such a weakling. Why doesn't he pull himself together?' She never could understand anyone who fell short of her exacting standards. She couldn't forgive either her father or Ben for 'letting her down', as she put it. Finally, Ben went away and only came back about twelve years ago, living as you see him now."

"What a tragic story."

"Yes, sometimes life can really defeat people who're not strong."

"Somehow, Ben has survived. He must have developed an inner core of resilience. Built a wall in there, or something."

"Yes, I think so."

Angela stood. "I have something — I wasn't going to show anyone, but now I think I must show you." She produced a piece of paper. "It was left with the empty thermos a few days ago. It's from Ben. I know you said you didn't want to read Miss Brooks's letters, but this is different. I think you should."

Pat read aloud:

"When sunsets die, and twilights fall,
If I tell of the heartbreaks there have been
Then see the freedom of the sky.
How grateful he should be,
To hear the cuckoo call."

There was silence as she finished reading, but Pat's eyes were full of tears when she looked up, as were Angela's.

CHAPTER 22

As if to make up for the harsh and bitter winter, spring burst into the river valley. The quarry was filled with frothing blackthorn blossom, and young grass speared upward through the dank soil. The trees had a mist of pale green, too, as new leaves began to sprout from tight buds.

Angela decided to keep Pat's revelations regarding Ben and Miss Brooks to herself. She needed to evaluate what she had learned, but she made up her mind that she would go on feeding and caring for Ben for as long as she was able. She didn't know if she was doing a wise thing, encouraging him from his isolation. If, for any reason, she was unable to maintain her support, he would be left in a worse predicament than before, but she refused to think along pessimistic lines. He was increasingly disposed to hold conversations. She discovered he had considerable knowledge on many subjects, though much was outdated or coloured by his own interpretations. Sometimes he made strange comments.

"Aren't you worried your car tyres might catch fire?" he asked unexpectedly one day. She was growing accustomed to his occasional lapses into his own world and tried to treat them with serious but balanced calm.

"Why should that happen?"

"With the roads so burning hot like this." He looked surprised and she noted that his eyes held an odd, blank expression. "Makes my feet so damn sore," he continued. "Pardon my language. It's them electricity pylons. Don't know why people have to have 'em."

"Try walking on the grass. It's cooler," she suggested. "My car tyres won't catch fire. They're insulated."

"Ah, that's good. Good." A moment later, he remarked in a normal way, "Soon be time for the cuckoos to come along. I like to hear them calling across the quarry to each other."

"*To hear the cuckoo call*," she quoted in an undertone. "Write me another poem, Ben. That one was very fine."

"I will." He nodded. "Sometime. Got to go now. Things to do."

He invariably ended their chats with that ritual sentence. She never tried to stop him leaving.

Whenever she went to the village shop, she made an effort to be pleasant to Miss Brooks, but her attempts at friendliness were met with monosyllabic replies and the postmistress kept her eyes lowered as she served.

Perhaps, Angela thought, she was embarrassed, remembering her behaviour when she'd shouted at her for helping Ben Cooper. Maybe she'd guessed someone must have told her the sad little story by now and resented the thought of Angela knowing. Probably Pat was right in saying she was spoilt from the start by overindulgent parents. How easy it was to make children's lives unhappy, even with the best of intentions.

Angela sighed and wondered again if she were handling Grace's adolescence in the best way. At least she and Ade would have discussed these things, even if their marriage hadn't worked in other ways. At present, Grace was as happy as a skylark. She and Q were preparing their small boat for the summer season and an April Easter Sunday re-launching. Debs, when she took time off from work, seemed subdued. Angela watched her covertly. She was fairly certain she had not been a regular at Home Farm since the return of the goose in January. Certainly, there had been no phone calls requesting

Debs's veterinary skills. Angela was still unsure about her daughter's feelings for Alan but had too little nerve to ask.

If Debs did want Alan, it looked as though she would have to make some decisive moves, and Angela was uncomfortably certain that her daughter's pride wouldn't allow that. But with their shared love of animals and ability to cope with difficulties, Angela thought they could form a strong partnership.

In early April, Debs received a letter with a French postmark. Jeannette Garot wrote that she and her mother planned to come to England at the end of the month. They would spend a few days in Waterthorpe, if that was still all right, then go to London. Jeannette had visited England before, but this was Madame Garot's first trip across the Channel and she was anxious to see the sights of the capital, apparently.

"I hope you're not regretting saying they could come at any time?" Debs asked her mother.

"Of course not. You said that Jeannette is keen to see your vet's practice. I just hope I can find enough to interest Madame Garot."

"She's used to country life. For a change, take her to Peterborough and show her the cathedral and the shopping centre. She'll like that."

"Yes, I will."

Privately, Angela was wishing she hadn't urged Debs to include Jeannette's mother in the invitation. At the time she had been desperately seeking a new distraction herself. Debs said Madame Garot could speak reasonable English. Angela's own French was pitiable. She'd hardly used it since her long-ago school days.

She also remembered that Madame Garot had hinted to Debs about some scandal to do with Gilles and his family.

Perhaps she should warn him of their impending arrival, she thought, but then she was overcome with anxieties. She didn't want him to think she was seeking confidences if she brought the subject up with him. If Gilles had anything he wished to hide, it was his own business. Grace had said he refused to talk with Q about their old life in France. What on earth could have happened there?

CHAPTER 23

At Christmas, Gilles had promised Q he would begin teaching him to drive a car as soon as the roads became less icy, but it was the middle of April before the lessons started.

"Prepare to turn left," Gilles said to his grandson. "Slow down; the turning is on the bridge, not after it. Slow down, Q. Slow DOWN."

"I am!"

They slid around the corner, crossing the white line to the wrong side before regaining the correct position on the road.

"I told you to go slower. It's lucky nothing was coming the other way." Gilles glanced across to see Q's glowering face. "You have to do as I say. That was a tricky situation there. We were very lucky."

"You said already," Q muttered.

They drove on in silence, which was fine as the road was long and straight. Gilles looked in the wing mirror and saw a car behind.

"Maybe a little faster. Up to the speed limit would be good. Twenty-five miles an hour will make people behind impatient."

"You said 'slow down' before," Q huffed.

"Yes, but that was going around a sharp corner."

"You need to tell me more clearly. And don't shout."

"Calm down. It's early days."

"Yes, it is."

It wasn't long before Gilles clasped his forehead and said, "Slow down for this bend."

"I'm getting out. I'll walk back. This is impossible. *You* are impossible." Q slammed the car door shut and stormed along the footpath.

Gilles got out and shouted, "Q, come back. This won't do. You'll be fine. Come on."

Q steadfastly ignored him, and Gilles watched as he shoved his hands into his pockets and strode away.

"Ah, *mon Dieu!*" Gilles threw both hands in the air before turning and climbing into the driver's seat.

He sat and gathered his thoughts. Had he been too harsh? The lad needed to be safe. He had to learn that what his grandfather said was correct. Gilles thumped the steering wheel and expelled a great gust of air.

He cruised the car slowly up to his grandson and, lowering the window, he called out as he came level. "Q, please, get in."

"No. You're impossible. You always think you're right."

Gilles was struck by the irony of his own thoughts being repeated back to him and allowed himself half a smile. "Okay, okay. I'm sorry. Come on, get in and I'll drive us home. You can go tell Grace how impossible I am."

Grace opened the door to Q when he came to Slater's Cottage with a thundercloud face immediately following this third lesson. He shared what had happened with her.

"He does nothing but shout and contradict himself. It's impossible." He flung himself into a chair, put his chin in his hand and scowled across the room.

Angela drew Grace aside and asked the reason.

"Q says Gilles gets so ratty and impatient," Grace said. "Q's trying his best, but oh, I don't know. Actually, Mum, I think they're six and two threes, the pair of them. They do seem to fight a lot, but they're as bad as each other."

"Generation gap, perhaps. Gilles's a good driver, very cool and competent, but I sometimes think he expects too much of Q too quickly, in a number of ways."

"I like Gilles," Grace said, looking defensive, "but it takes everybody ages to learn how to drive, doesn't it?"

"A few months, usually, sometimes more."

"They had this awful row this morning." Grace looked dismal. "Q got out of the car and swore he wouldn't learn from his *grandpère* any longer. Eventually Q got back in the car and Gilles drove back."

"Oh dear," said Angela. "That bad already, is it?"

"I don't know what Q will do now. He's simply dying to pass his test, so we can borrow the car and drive out. He's planning to sell his motorbike and save for a car of his own."

"Is he indeed? Well, I dare say Gilles is regretting having had harsh words too," Angela said in a dry tone. "He thinks everyone ought to be able to drive and he's very keen for Q to do well. That's part of the trouble, I think."

Grace gazed at her pleadingly. "Do you think you can talk to Gilles, Mum?"

"If you'll tell Q to have patience," Angela said, "I might try."

She sent Q and Grace out for a walk with Ranger to give the boy a chance to cool his temper.

"I'll make myself a coffee while you're gone and have a think about the best way forwards."

She had switched the kettle on and put the coffee in a mug when there was a knock at the door.

"Angelique, I must speak with you. Is the boy still here?" Gilles tried to peer around her.

"He and Grace have taken Ranger out. Come inside, Gilles. I was just making a coffee. Do you want one?"

In the living room he turned to face her, looking a little sheepish. "I suppose he has told you that we quarrelled?"

"He told Grace. She's said something about it to me."

"It is my fault," Gilles said. "Me, I have little patience, and it angers me when Q answers impertinently when I try to teach him."

"Perhaps if he had a few lessons first with a driving school?" Angela said.

"I have thought of it, but it costs a great deal. Q already knows about my car, and I think he learns easily. It is a matter of some practice, but with someone who possesses a patient disposition to sit beside him. Alas, I realise that I have not."

"There's a simple solution. I'll sit next to him. He can practise in my car."

Gilles gazed at her in evident horror. "But no, my dear Angelique, I could not allow such a thing. I did not mean you, when I spoke. For you to be responsible while Q learns… It is too dangerous."

"Rubbish!" Angela laughed a little to soften the exclamation. "I'm perfectly capable. I sat with Debs when she was learning. Ade had little patience. In my experience, the nicest men turn into fiends once they get inside a car with a learner."

Gilles smiled faintly but still shook his head. "I couldn't let you take such risks."

"Q is old enough to drive, and he and I get along well. I'm sure he'll do as I tell him. He's not as close to me so he won't be awkward, I'm sure. I'm going to teach Grace in the autumn, as soon as she's seventeen."

"That I cannot forbid, alas, but…" All at once, Gilles took her hands, holding them to his chest. "What should I do, my dearest Angelique, if there was an accident? You are now so very necessary to my life."

"Gilles, really, I…" She realised suddenly that she was being plunged headlong into the thing she had been carefully avoiding since Christmas.

He interrupted her. "No. Now you must let me speak; let me say this to you. I have waited because I understood that you needed more time to recover from the death of your husband. I have had longer to grow accustomed to life without my Marie. And for a while, I thought Alan…" He smiled at his own foolishness.

"Gilles, please…"

"Permit me to finish, *chérie*. You and I, we are two lonely people. You have your daughters but no man. I have Q, but… It's not just a convenience for our children. Now I care for you also, Angelique. Very deeply, I care for you. I need you."

"We're … we're good friends."

"Friendship is not enough. Not for me. I am sixty-one years old, but I can make you happy. We can be a success together. Surely you have realised, have known I would ask if you would have me?"

"I have thought about it, but…"

He let go of her hands. "But you do not care for me as I care for you. Perhaps I was right, that it is Alan for whom you care."

"Alan? No! Never him. I do care for you, and maybe I do even love you. But I don't know if we can be together."

"Angelique, why not?"

"It's Grace. Oh, she likes you, a lot. She's told me so, more than once. But … it may be difficult for you to understand. Oh dear." She took a deep breath and plunged on. "Grace and Q also have deep emotions for each other. I know they're young, but not too young to fall in love. Grace says it would be impossible for her and Q if we were, you know…"

"This is ridiculous. Must we stay apart because of some immature feelings they imagine they have? They fall in love now, or so they think, but surely it must be only — what is it? The love of calves?"

"Calf love, perhaps." A small smile played around the corners of her lips.

"Next year, the year after, they will fall out of love. It happens constantly at their age."

"I know. It's probably true. I've tried to warn Grace, but she can't believe it at the moment."

Gilles sighed with impatience. "You and I, Angelique, especially I, have no time to waste for this. I want you, my love, and I will always find ways to make you happy. I swear that I will look after you until the end of my life."

"I know, Gilles. I know you would."

He looked into her eyes and saw her unhappiness.

"I don't know what to do for the best. I don't want to hurt you, but I won't hurt Grace. She's had such a lot to cope with since Ade's passing. I promised her I wouldn't do anything she doesn't like. And she doesn't want me to have another relationship again. Not right now."

"This is madness. I cannot accept this. I must speak with her."

"No, no, you mustn't."

Gilles opened his arms and Angela moved towards him. He caught her against him and as his arms encircled her slim shoulders, his desire intensified. He leaned down to kiss her gently.

Her lips were warm and yielding as the stiffness left her body. He was aware of every tingling nerve, every soft movement. The slow slide of warmth on warmth, sighing joy and pleasure. Gently he moved so that he wouldn't scare her, vaguely aware that he pulled her body against his own with one arm, while the other hand cradled her head. She shuddered beneath his caress. An echo in the pit of his stomach nearly overwhelmed him. Somehow, with a groan and extreme self-discipline, he released her and turned away.

He heard her soft voice. "Perhaps the fact that her happiness is more important to me than yours, *ours*, is sufficient reason for me to refuse you."

He nodded. Without turning to look at her again, he moved to the door, but he heard panic in her next words.

"But we can still remain friends, can't we? Please, can we be friends?"

Then he turned. "If that is what you wish."

As he opened the door and stepped out, she followed him.

"There's something I wanted to tell you."

He looked at her.

"Debs's French friends, the Garots, are coming here next week. Jeannette Garot is a vet like Debs. She's coming with her mother. They live in St André de la Marche. Isn't that where you used to live?"

" Yes, that is where I am from."

With that, he turned and strode away. As he made his way home, his devastation at Angelique's words deepened. How could they stay friends? He loved her too intensely.

And now the Garots were coming — another problem to worry about. Perhaps he should have told Q the family secret years ago, when he was still very young. But then he would have had to live with that weight on his shoulders. He had been too young to understand what was being said on television. He wouldn't have been aware of newspapers. The knowing stares and the nods and comments of neighbours had been fleeting because he, Gilles, had taken the necessary steps to get them safely to England. Q had therefore been spared the stigma of his father's betrayal.

Perhaps he shouldn't have chosen this small place, twinned with St André de la Marche, but in his haste, he knew of no other area where he could have found work and accommodation with ease. He'd done farm labouring for some time before the gardener's job came up at Moondreams House, and Gatekeeper's Cottage also became available. When the head gardener retired, Gilles took over the responsibility for the grounds and was now developing the gardens further.

Surely shielding Q from all that they had run from was the right thing. The boy may never need to hear about it. But now these people were coming from his old village, bringing it all to the surface again. His secrets would become a cloud of whispers spreading like dandelion seeds on a breeze. He ran his hand through his hair and sighed.

Maybe they need not meet. Surely Madame Garot and her daughter would not be here for long. Perhaps he could keep Q away for those days. Keep him busy around the gardens; ensure he had no time to go and see Grace and bump into them. Yes, that must be the best plan.

His mind darted back inexorably to his main concern. Angelique. Did she mean she would come to him eventually, perhaps when the children were older and had outgrown their teenage infatuation?

His mind wandered on. Should he let her give Q a driving lesson? The very thought made him shudder. What if Q did something stupid and endangered both their lives? That would be unbearable.

A short while later, Gilles was sitting at the table in the living room with an espresso in front of him, hoping the concentrated caffeine would help. There were jobs to be done, and he made a move to get on. He couldn't afford to sit there feeling sorry for himself. As he thought this, he heard the sound of Q's motorbike.

Q's shown no interest in that for months, Gilles thought as he looked up and then hastened to the door. He was in time to see a wisp of blue and hear the roar as Q gunned the motorbike down the narrow road. He was going too fast. He hadn't been that impetuous for a long time. Now what? There was no point texting or phoning him if he was on the bike.

He returned to the table, gulped his coffee, and headed outside to do some routine work. Perhaps that would take his mind off things.

It was some time later when Gilles looked at his watch. It was lunchtime, so he hurried home to see what Q had been up to. Silence. He dug his phone out of his pocket and rang Q's number. No reply.

He paced for a minute and then put the omelette pan on the range. It was unlike his grandson to miss a meal. He reached for his phone again and tapped in Angela's number.

"Hello. It's Gilles. Is Q with you? I need to have him home."

"No. He hasn't been here since he and Grace returned with Ranger. If you haven't seen him, you won't have heard. They arrived back full of it."

"What now?" He was irritated. Trouble followed that boy. He had thought he was growing up at last. "Tch!"

"They were talking to Jack Marsh up the road — the community policeman. He told them there was an application to let the far side of the quarry, the small part that isn't David's, to be used by a motorcycle club eight Sundays each year. For scramble races."

"And Q was excited by that, I suppose? Honestly!"

"No, no, not at all. He was as horrified as Grace and I. In fact, he was really angry about it. It'll wreck the wildlife there. They'll stamp all over the bee orchids. Probably not even notice them. And the magnificent deer will be scared away. It was the thought of the wildlife that really made him cross. And Ben…" She said no more.

"That sounds terrible, I agree. But where would Q have gone?"

"He said something about the planning office at the Town Hall in Peterborough. That's not all. There's a proposal for it to be made into a national scrambling centre. The hills and hollows are the perfect terrain, apparently. That would mean motorbikes every weekend and practising on some weekdays too."

"It does sound appalling. Our road systems wouldn't take all the extra traffic either. I'm sure it would be a safety issue."

"And hotdog stands and ice-cream vans with motorbikes buzzing up and down the street on their way to the pub…" Angela lamented. "What I'm really concerned about is Ben. He'll hate the noise and all those people. He'll be scared witless. It might be enough to drive him away, and he depends on us now."

"What do you mean?"

Angela sighed. "I might as well confess. I told Pat the other day anyway." She told him she'd been feeding the rough sleeper and even mentioned the poem that Ben had given her, justifying her actions by referring to the appalling weather they'd had over the winter. Gilles heard the break in her voice and wanted to wrap his arms around her.

Then there was a bang on his door. "Sorry, I must go," he said. "Someone's at the door. Thank you, Angelique. Please do not worry. If you see Q, would you ask him to come straight home, please?"

"Yes, of course. Bye."

Gilles disconnected the call and put the phone back in his pocket as he headed along the hallway.

His stomach dropped as he opened the door. He stood holding on to it to stop his knees from giving way. There stood a policewoman, with a notebook in her hand and a worried expression on her face.

CHAPTER 24

"It's just awful," Grace said to her mum. "Q couldn't see it at first. He was going on about the excitement of a motorbike club. He said it might bring this place alive."

"Did he think he might go up there and join in?" asked Angela.

"I told him right then that I wouldn't be going with him, but he said it was a private club, so he wouldn't be able to anyhow."

"What's he up to now?"

"When he stopped to think about it, he got quite cross. He's gone to the Town Hall to find out exactly what's going on. He was already in a bad mood about the driving lessons, and this didn't help."

"I hope he'll be careful, then. The last thing Gilles needs right now is for him to come to grief."

"I'm going to start a petition," Grace said, "and I'm going to write letters to whoever I can think of. Will you give me a hand?"

"Yes, I certainly will. Gilles said something about our roads not being up to it and the extra traffic being a safety issue, so that's some more departments we can target." Angela headed for her study. "If you make a start on designing a petition, I'll draft some letters."

The activity masked some of her anxiety about Gilles and his earlier visit. She stared across the top of her laptop, not seeing the garden, the blue sky, the birds as they hopped and twittered on the opposite roofs. The subsequent conversation on the telephone had played out as if nothing had been said, no declaration made, adding to her confusion and guilt. In the months since she'd seen Ade with the redhead, she had lurched from one guilt trip to the next. Now here she was again, just as her confidence and certainty were returning. Her self-condemnation seemed to know no bounds but, surely, she was right to consider Grace before herself and Gilles. She was still a child and was her sole responsibility. There seemed to be no way around the fact that Grace didn't want her to have a full-blown relationship with anyone, never mind the father of her boyfriend. Would Gilles still want her in say, four or five years, when Grace had left home? Would she still want him? Anything might happen in that time.

The phone in her pocket buzzed and drew her away from her thoughts. Glancing at the display, she saw that Gilles was calling again. She was tempted not to answer but eventually accepted the call.

"Angelique. Oh, Angelique. Thank goodness you are there. I need to speak with you."

His voice was fraught and a chill ran through her.

"What is it? What's the matter?" All her troubles evaporated as she caught the tenor of his anxiety.

"It's Q."

"What? Tell me." She tried to sound calm. "Gilles, tell me what's wrong."

There was a tremor, and he cleared his throat. Then his voice was stronger. "He had an accident. On the A1. He's in hospital. Came off his motorbike."

"Oh my… Where are you? I'll come. Is he…? Is he alive, Gilles?" The air left her body. Her knees shook. Her hand became clammy.

"He's in a coma. He's alive. He has broken bones in both arms. We're at Peterborough." She heard a strangled sob and a gasp.

"I'm coming."

"Oh yes, please. Be careful."

How to tell Grace that her love was hurt so badly? And in another motorbike accident. Oh God! What if… How would her child manage this? She fell back into the chair and a tear escaped and rolled down her cheek. She dashed it away and straightened her shoulders.

"Grace, can you come here a moment?"

Her daughter came thundering down the stairs and into the tiny study. She stopped, becoming abruptly aware of her mother's serious expression.

"Darling, something's happened. It'll be fine, though." Angela knew the futility of her reassurances. She stood and reached out. Grace came into the circle of her arms. "It's Q," she whispered into her hair. "He's come off his motorbike."

"No!"

As Grace pulled away and looked up, Angela held her shoulders and stared into her eyes, summoning every ounce of her strength. "He'll be okay, I'm sure. He's alive. He's in the hospital, but he's alive. Darling Grace. He'll be all right. This is different. It may take a little time, that's all."

Their tears mingled as Angela kissed Grace's cheek and held her close.

"I'm coming, too," she said.

"No, darling. They won't let you in. They may not let me in either. Come with me next door and we'll tell Pat. She'll make sure you're okay. I'll go and find out more. I'll ring you from the hospital when I know what's going on. Maybe you can visit soon. I'll be home later."

CHAPTER 25

When Gilles appeared at the far end of the corridor, he saw Angela's anxious face through the small window as she waited beyond the door.

He spread his arms and she took shelter, her head resting on his chest. His heart beat faster. She must hear it, surely, as it raced when he encircled her. She stood back and looked up at him.

"Tell me," she said softly, without preamble.

"It was one of those turnings across the A1. They've closed a lot of them off, but at this one a truck was trying to come off the northbound onto the southbound carriageway. Q hit the side of it as it pulled out. It wasn't even Q's fault, couldn't have been. It was his right of way. He's got a small brain bleed, but it's his liver. It's lacerated badly. He's in a medically induced coma."

Angela closed her eyes for a moment and took a deep breath. "Why have they done that? I thought they only did that for severe brain trauma."

Gilles's thoughts ran. *Mon Dieu, this must be hell for her, after what she has been through*, he thought. And yet she'd come to him without hesitation. "I think it allows his brain to shut down a bit, to rest, so his body can heal and doesn't have to work hard to retain all the functions. They do that for him with machines. I don't really understand it all." He put his head on her shoulder, helplessness overwhelming him.

"Does he have other injuries?" Her voice was soft with concern. His left arm remained around her slim waist.

"He's broken his left arm and his right wrist is fractured. They haven't set those yet. He's bruised a lung, and a kidney has damage but that can repair itself, apparently. They're trying to make sure his liver is going to heal, and the brain bleed is under control. His arms took the full force of the impact. Otherwise, it would have been his head, or neck and spine. He could have been killed or paralysed. Oh God, why did I let him have a motorbike? I was so stupid. I should have insisted." Tears welled in his eyes again.

"Hush now." Angela stretched up and her soft lips brushed his cheek. "He's so lucky he wasn't run over from behind. He's alive." She stroked the back of his head. "He's here. He has you with him, and I'm here for you."

"I need to get back. Come with me? Please." He took her hands in his.

"If they'll let me. I'm not a relative."

He rang the bell, and the nurse came and ushered them both through the door, indicating the antiseptic gel dispenser just inside.

"He's got breathing tubes and all sorts of monitors and machines making noises." Gilles took her hand, linking his fingers through hers.

The other five beds were empty, so Q had the full attention of the nurses available. As he hadn't been in there long, Gilles was pleased about this, but his boy looked small and lonely. His limbs were encased in what looked like blow-up bags, supporting his broken bones. Thin tubes were up his nose and thicker ones in his mouth. Some sort of aspirator was breathing for him, and a catheter ran from under the covers to a bag hanging from the side of the bed. Another bag hanging from a stand was connected to tubes that ran to his arm. Gilles was grateful for Angela's warm fingers laced through his own, until he let go to stroke Q's hair from his forehead and whisper words of encouragement and love.

"Can he hear us?" Angela addressed the nurse who was hovering nearby.

"He won't remember much but yes, he can probably hear you. It's good to talk quietly and calmly to him and to hold his hand. And remember, he won't be feeling pain while we have him under. That's another advantage when healing the brain and, in his case, the liver."

Later, Angela returned home and updated Grace. "It's early and difficult to say, but Q might only be in a coma for four or five days." She wrapped her arms around her daughter as they stood in the kitchen. Then, producing a clean tissue from her pocket, she wiped away her tears. "He's alive. He's very lucky. They think he'll make a complete recovery."

Fresh tears rolled down Grace's cheeks. Debs had come home, listened to the details and hugged her mother with fervour. Angela was so grateful she cried then, too. Then her older daughter disappeared down the road, saying she had some animal medication to deliver to Alan at Home Farm. To the best of Angela's knowledge, Debs hadn't seen the farmer in a while. Or perhaps she had, and her mother hadn't noticed because she'd had so much going on in her own head.

Angela visited the hospital each day. On the third occasion, she took Grace, who was allowed a quick visit because it was so quiet and the rules in the ICU were at the nurses' discretion. Angela stepped back as Grace held Q's hand and spoke to him. Gilles came to stand beside her.

"How are you coping?" She looked up at his face and touched his arm, noting the pallid hue to his normally brown complexion.

He regarded her. "Better for seeing you and having your support. They're talking about possibly starting to reduce the medication in another day or two, but they're still not able to say when exactly."

"How long will it take for him to wake up?"

"Apparently he's on something called Propofol. It's like a foreign language. Anyway, it's used in cases of so-called 'soft' admission in here. He should start to wake up quite quickly. Maybe twelve to twenty-four hours, once they start the process. They'll take him off the ventilator then, too." He rubbed each eye and heaved a great sigh.

"You're exhausted," Angela said. "Why don't you go home and get some proper rest? I'll stay, if you like. Nothing's going to happen yet, not until they do start reducing the meds. Take Grace with you."

"Really? I don't know. I want to stay."

"I know you do, but he'll need you when he finally wakes up. You'll be no use if you've made yourself ill. I'll call you if there is any change at all. You know I will. Take a taxi. Don't try and drive."

"That makes sense." He laughed ruefully. "All right. Angelique, you are my saviour. What would I do without you in my life?"

Fire shot through her as she listened. Managing to steady her voice, she called, "Grace, Gilles and you are to take a taxi home. I'll be there later. Debs will look after you. I'll ring her." She turned back to Gilles and reached up to kiss his roughened cheek. "Take care," she whispered. Then to Grace, "Go and finish your posters and petition. We'll take them around the village tomorrow."

"I don't want to go," she said.

"I know, but the task at home will keep you busy and stop you worrying. Q is in safe hands, and he'll be well soon. Don't let him down, darling girl."

Grace frowned, but her face cleared as she bent to Q and whispered to him, before letting go of his hand and walking to the door of the ICU, where she waited for Gilles.

Gilles took Angela's hands in his own and kissed first one and then the other. "*Mon cœur*, no matter what you say," he said softly, before turning away.

She had no time to say anything in response, but she watched as they retreated along the corridor. At the door, they each turned. Grace gave a self-conscious little wave and Gilles blew her a kiss.

Once they'd gone, Angela sat beside Q's bed, reaching out to stroke the hair away from his forehead.

"Get well, sweetheart. Your grandad and Grace need you. Now probably more than ever."

Angela's thoughts rambled on silently as she remembered that Jeannette Garot and her mother were visiting imminently. She didn't know what had happened back in France, before Gilles and his family had come here, but she did know that the boy's grandfather thought the world of him and didn't want past troubles to wreck the lad's peace here. It must have been much more than an affair, or Q's father running off and leaving them all. When she got home, perhaps she would have a look on the internet. Before, it had seemed disloyal, but how could she prepare if she didn't know? She'd never tell Gilles she'd looked.

She sat back and closed her eyes.

When Angela awoke, she was still holding Q's hand, and Gilles was coming towards her. She glanced at her watch, feeling sheepish.

"It's not been very long."

"I had a proper shower and a shave. I slept for an hour and a half, but it seemed like five. I think I must have been out like a light, as you say, and slept deeply. I feel better, anyway. Thank you so much, my Angelique." He put his arms out and as she stepped towards him, he folded them around her, and her head rested in the hollow beneath his shoulder. Why was life so complicated?

Angela needed to tell him she loved him. She wanted to let him know that whatever was in his past was of no consequence. She was on the verge of saying it, but too much was going on. Q must return to them first. Their children were their priority.

CHAPTER 26

Debs peered over her younger sister's shoulder. "What's that you're doing?"

"I've made some sheets for a petition. Q and I were going to go around the houses here and take some to the other local villages too."

"You can't do all that on your own," Debs said.

"I know. Mum said she'd help. I know she's drafted some letters to various departments at the Town Hall." Grace pointed at her mother's laptop. "Q was going to help me, but…"

"I'm not working today or tomorrow morning. I'll give you a hand."

"Really?"

"Yes. If this scrambling idea takes off, it'll affect us all. I think Alan might help too. He knows a lot of the farmers around here. I can't imagine any of them will like the idea, and some of them are quite powerful on the Council."

Grace was surprised and grateful to her sister. Together, they did the round of the village with Grace's petition and received only three refusals to sign. These came from folk who were planning to let their gardens as carparks and make some money.

"But I think they'll have their own carpark facilities on site," Grace tried, but she couldn't think of a comeback when the people said they would be cheaper.

"It's not that we begrudge other people enjoying their hobby," Grace explained in earnest to those who were reluctant to sign. "We just think it will spoil our wildlife. There are one or two quite rare plants growing in the quarry, too. Just imagine if it's developed into a major scrambling centre. No more Sunday peace. There are fewer and fewer places left now where animals can flourish undisturbed, or people can go for a quiet walk on weekends."

"I don't think our road system is up to the extra traffic either," Debs added. "They'll have to widen certain parts or build a new entrance. Either way, it will mean muck and noise. It's certainly not safe as it is at the moment."

They plodded on before going back to Debs's car to head to the next village.

"I think some people signed the petition because they like you and feel sorry for Q," Debs said in her forthright way.

"Oh, don't say that. Surely, they can see the sense in the argument. We need them to be genuine." Grace was aware of the resentment in her voice and guessed that Debs must have heard it too.

"Yes, of course. I'm sorry. You're doing a great job."

Harmony restored, they covered the next village and gained many more signatures. Some people were not at home, so they made a note to return later.

"Right, we'll go to Alan's and talk to him. He'll probably give us a drink. I'm ready for one," Debs stated.

Grace wasn't sure she wanted to go there, but Debs had been so kind that she said nothing as she drove them back to their own village and turned into Alan Cooper's yard.

The smell of cows was strong, but all was clean as Grace opened the car door.

"He should be around at this time of day. He usually has a break before milking," Debs said with an authority about which Grace wondered. Her sister seemed to know a lot about

Alan's routines. Her mind turned faster as Debs tried the door and, finding it unlocked, went straight in. "Hello," she called.

There was no response, so Grace hung back as Debs marched down the hallway. She returned a moment later. "He's not here," she said. "Let's try the barn."

Grace scuttled out and as Debs emerged from the house, Alan came from around the corner.

"Oh, hello," he said. "I thought I heard your car."

He recognises the sound of her engine, Grace thought.

As Debs stood on her toes and leaned in to kiss his cheek, Grace was aware of her own face flaming. What was going on here? This was a turn-up. She supposed she'd been wrapped up in her own stuff and hadn't noticed.

Alan flicked a glance at her and then looked down at Debs and smiled. He listened with keen attention while she described their activities. "Come in and have a cup of tea," he said. Again, his eyes darted to Grace and left quickly as he led the way to the house. Grace followed with reluctance. She wasn't sure about this at all.

They sat around the table in the gloomy kitchen. Grace played with her fingers and kept her head down. From time to time, she peeked up to see a pile of magazines on a small table next to a scruffy chair; some plates left to drain next to the sink; a weird contraption up near the ceiling with what appeared to be a rope and pulley system to raise and lower it. It had socks hanging on the slatted wood.

Thank goodness there was no underwear. Big boxers or, even worse, large white Y-fronts would be the end. She'd die. Wait until she told Q. He'd crease up. She wished he was there. Her tummy tightened and she sighed.

Embarrassment took hold when she realised Debs had addressed her and she hadn't heard a word.

"Grace, get a grip," her sister said. "Alan, say all that again for the sake of my dumb sister."

"I was saying," he began as he turned away to fill the cups, "well … I was at the quarry on Sunday morning. Took Jip up there. I heard this buzzing sound." He turned to Debs. "Started off like a low humming, then it grew louder, like a swarm of gigantic angry bees."

Grace was surprised by how much Alan spoke to her sister. He never normally had two words to rub together, or whatever the saying was. She had to admit that he looked different when he smiled at Debs. It lit up his face. Crinkles appeared at the corners of his eyes, and he looked quite charming. Well, sort of. He continued, and Grace snapped her mind to attention.

"As I came out of the woods, there was a tannoy blaring orders to riders. There were a few local people standing and watching. There were stakes bashed into the ground, setting out a track, and several riders lined up for the start of what was a race, by the look of it. I know old Ben lives up there, but there was no sign of him."

"Did you see them racing?" Grace asked, forgetting her reserve.

"Oh yes." He looked away from her. "About six bikes started up at the same time. It was a deafening roar." He looked at Debs.

"It'll be devastation in no time," Debs said.

"Q said it was only a proposition. He must be wrong." Grace was angry now and spoke loudly. "It'll only be a short while before a National Centre becomes fact."

"Surely they could use a track at a stadium somewhere," said Debs. "What about the Showground? It's further away from residential areas and there's no wildlife. Much safer access. Everything. Mmm, no hills and hollows, though, I suppose."

They chatted further. Grace noticed that Alan spoke to Debs more naturally than she had ever seen him speak to anyone. Debs laughed at what he said, smiled at him.

If Debs moved out and came down here, thought Grace, she could have her room, which was bigger and lighter. Or her mum could turn it into her new study, and she and Q could turn her present study into a sitting room for themselves. They could paint it up, have a little sofa and a TV. Perfect. With thoughts of Q her tummy contracted, and she had a sudden shiver of fear.

"Come on, Grace. Time to go. Wait in the car. I'll be out in a mo," said Debs.

Grace gave her a look but decided she didn't want to witness what might follow. Her imagination was enough.

CHAPTER 27

Yet again, Gilles told Angela how grateful he was.

"I cannot manage without you," he said as she came into his arms and her head rested in the hollow beneath his shoulder. He kissed her sweet-smelling hair, taking comfort from her warmth. After a moment, she drew back.

"I... Never mind. Now is not the time."

She became business-like. Was she still frightened of his feelings for her? He didn't know. Gilles needed her like he had needed no other, not even his Marie. That had been young love and they were close, but this, this was mature and needy in a such a different way. He watched as Angela walked away from him, then sat and took Q's hand.

As he watched the boy's sleeping form and tried to ignore the whooshing and bleeping sounds of the machines, there was a quiet flurry of movement in his peripheral vision. Mr Johnson, the consultant, had arrived with a couple of others in white coats. The nurses left their station and they all gathered around the bed. Gilles rose from his seat and listened intently.

"Tomorrow we will reduce his medication and encourage him to wake," said Mr Johnson. "The last scan was positive. I have every expectation that all will be fine, Mr Richard, and that your grandson will make a full recovery. However, we shall know more tomorrow. I advise that you go home and have a proper sleep. He will need you tomorrow." He turned to one of the white coats. "Dr Thomas, here, will explain what may happen. In the meantime, I wish you a good night, Mr Richard, and we'll see Q tomorrow." With that he shook Gilles's hand, turned, and left with all except Dr Thomas.

"It's not uncommon for a patient to wake up and feel disorientated. He has probably been able to hear much of what has been said to him but may only remember bits of it. He may wonder why he's here at all."

"I see."

"Sometimes we have to administer more medication to put a patient under again and bring him around more slowly, if he appears too stressed or is panicking. We'll see how we go on that. Don't be too worried. I know it all sounds a bit frightening and its's new to you, but we've done this many, many times before."

"What about his broken bones?"

"We'll set those in a day or two, when he's fully conscious again. No harm done there, to have left it a bit. The bones are supported in these bags. We needed to get the liver laceration and the internal bruising sorted out and under control. Go home, Mr Richard. As Mr Johnson says, Q will need you tomorrow."

"I suppose I could."

"He won't wake tonight. The meds will see to that. He'll need you in the morning, fully rested."

When Dr Thomas had gone, Gilles sat again with Q. "I'm going home for a while, my dearest boy. I shall be back in the morning. Rest now. All will be well," he said, to reassure himself as much as Q.

When Gilles got home, he rang Angela and told her they were going to encourage his boy to awaken the next day.

"That's such good news."

He smiled gently at the warmth in her voice and ran his hand down the side of his face, the roughness reminding him of how tired he was.

"Take heart. It all sounds positive." There was a moment of silence. "Gilles, that other thing." There was another pause.

"What other thing?"

Then she spoke again. "Madame and Jeannette Garot."

"Ah, yes!" He tried to keep the exasperation and worry from his voice.

"I'm sorry to bring it up. I know it's the last thing you need to think about, but I've managed to put them off for a bit. I think they still will come, but not for a couple of weeks."

"Right. Thank you for letting me know." He knew he sounded stiff and formal. It would be better if they came right now, while Q was away, but he could hardly say that when Angela thought she was helping. She must be almost as tired as he, and probably didn't feel like having guests at all.

"Take care, my dear man."

"Oh, Angelique," was all he could say.

"Let me know how Q is tomorrow." Her voice, disembodied, sounded far away and he was so lonely.

"Yes, of course."

As they said their goodbyes, he straightened his shoulders and decided to go out and check on his greenhouses before he got some rest. Maybe a glass of wine before he slept, but just the one.

Outside and down the lane, he met Alan coming back from a walk with his dog. "How are things?" his friend asked.

Gilles shared the hospital news and then said, "To be honest, *mon ami*, I must tell you that Angela has been my anchor, my mainstay. I think you have a fancy for her, too, no?"

"Ha! Good Lord, no! Wherever did you get that idea? Her daughter, maybe. Debs. We have a lot in common, she and I." He looked at the ground and scuffed his toe in the dusty gravel. "She knows and loves animals. She is strong and determined and supports me in every way."

"But what about all the gifts, the flowers, the items you produce here, that you have given?"

"I thought perhaps Debs would think well of me for that." He smiled deprecatingly. "I've discussed that with her."

"And does Debs understand? We thought it was Angela that you had taken a fancy to. Are you getting it together with Debs?" Gilles gave a wide smile.

"Oh yes. We are doing very well, thank you." It was Alan's turn to grin, but sheepishly, and he looked at the toe of his shoe making sweeps in the gravel.

"Good luck, then, *mon ami*," Gilles said and clapped Alan on the shoulder.

"And to you, for tomorrow, with Q."

"Yes, thank you." Gilles's expression was sober before he continued on his way, thoughtful about the future.

The next day, Gilles sat holding his grandson's hand and waiting. The nurse had told him Q could come back to him at any moment. He also remembered and worried that they might need to put him under again if he woke up too confused and distressed. He rubbed his thumb across the back of Q's hand. God, he was so utterly weary.

He was looking down at their entwined hands when he became aware of a twitch, a mere tremble. Raising his eyes to Q's face, he leaned forward. He saw Q's eyes open and close again. Gilles leaned further, willing him to wake and be calm. Gently he put his hand on the boy's forehead and stroked his brow. Q's eyes opened, and this time he looked directly at Gilles.

"Oh, my dearest boy," Gilles whispered, and all the air left his lungs in a gush.

He received a feeble smile in return.

"Nurse," Gilles called softly. He looked back at Q. "I love you so much."

"And I you. I'm so sorry."

"Ssh."

The nurse arrived, and all became business-like.

When Q arrived home with plaster casts on his arms and looking pale, the village quietly rejoiced. Far from being the tiresome tearaway, he had gained a heroism befitting a long-lost son. People greeted him, asked after him, helped him to open doors, and generally coddled and protected him. He thanked them for their help with an impish grin. He tired easily, though, and Grace was solicitous in her attention to his well-being, which he also enjoyed a lot.

CHAPTER 28

The Garots were travelling from France on an early ferry. Angela could put them off no longer. After the ferry, they would take a train and eventually arrive in Peterborough in the early evening. Debs was taking two days off work and would drive into the city to meet them. Angela spent the weekend preparing for their arrival. It helped to take her mind off the fact that again, Gilles had failed to call her or visit for over a week, though Q was much better.

Had their conversation regarding Grace and her views on their developing relationship changed his mind? After all that had happened between then and now, it seemed things had reverted to how they had been. She had a lengthy baking session and beat her cake mixture with unusual violence as she thought about it all.

Angela decided to give up her bedroom to Madame Garot and accept the Singletons' offer for her to stay in their spare room. Grace would move in with Debs so that Jeannette could use her smaller room. She got rid of further bad thoughts as she thoroughly cleaned and polished things to within a gnat's whisker of their continuing existence.

When she saw Q, she asked in what she hoped was a casual tone, "Do you think your grandfather might come and visit this evening? He used to come on a Sunday, sometimes."

"He's in such a grumpy mood he's hardly spoken to me for two days," Q replied cheerfully. "Better left alone till he's got over whatever it is he has on his mind."

This was scarcely consoling.

"Are you staying for tea today?"

Q shook his head. "Can't today, but thanks anyway. *Grandpère* said he wants me home this evening. Said he has something he wants to talk to me about. Only hope it puts him in a better temper."

Even more unsettled, Angela slept badly. As the time approached for Debs to return from the station with the visitors, she found she was pacing the house with a knot in her stomach. She was sure she'd have nothing in common with Madame Garot.

When Debs's car drew up at the gate, she watched from behind the curtains. The guests came up the path. Madame Garot wore a plain black coat, and as she walked Angela could see a black skirt beneath. She had on a squashy black straw hat and strands of grey hair wisped about her thick neck. Her broad face and figure, her lack of chic style, spoke of French village life from a previous decade. Jeannette was also plump but seemed animated, talking over her shoulder to Debs, who was heaving their cases.

She's dressed for a funeral, Angela thought. *This will be a disaster.*

More and more she worried about whether she and Madame Garot would be able to converse with reasonable fluency. Debs spoke French quite well after her year's stay in France, but she and Jeannette would not be around much of the time. To Angela's relief, it soon became evident that Madame Garot did speak tolerable English, though with a marked accent. Neither did she seem overawed by her first visit to a foreign country and was extravagant in her praise of Angela's home. As she took off her coat and Angela hung it up, she saw that her blouse had huge red and purple flowers.

"Ah, but it is beautiful," she said on entering and looking around. When she went into Angela's bedroom and eyed the white duvet cover with its embroidered blue flowers and the matching curtains, she clasped her hands. "*Merveilleux!* You are kind." She laughed gently as she removed her hat and tossed it without ceremony onto the chair in the corner.

Angela judged that the lady enjoyed her lunch. Then, when Debs and Jeannette took themselves out for a car ride to see some of the countryside, she settled herself on the settee and dug in a cavernous bag to extricate a large ball of navy wool and knitting needles.

"I knit the woollen…" She plucked at the sleeve of her own cardigan.

"Ah, a cardigan?"

"Yes, but not these." She gestured to the buttons.

Angela chuckled and lifted her chin in understanding. "A jumper, then."

They both laughed again. So, the afternoon began to pass in a companionable way.

"You speak English well, *Madame*. Much better than I speak French," Angela said. At the back of her mind, she listened for the doorbell, which might herald the arrival of Q or even Gilles. She wondered how they would greet one another, this lady and him. "Did you only learn at school?"

"*Non.* And my name is Felice, please." Madame Garot shook her head with vigour. "My mother had an English friend who also lived in St André de la Marche. She teach us how to speak the language."

"An English lady?" Angela focused on the key interest among all this.

Felice Garot shrugged expressively. "An English lady, yes. Marie."

So, it was true. Gilles and his wife Marie were the Richards the Garots had known, and undoubtedly Felice Garot could explain the mystery in Gilles's background if Angela gave her the opportunity. Angela hovered between passionate curiosity and a deep reluctance to discover what it was that Gilles seemed anxious she should not learn.

CHAPTER 29

"Now that you are getting better, perhaps we will resume your driving lessons," Gilles said.

"But…"

"A moment." Gilles raised his hands, palms facing Q in surrender. "I propose that you have five lessons with a driving school, and then perhaps we will allow Angela to sit beside you for some extra practice."

The lad grinned. "Sounds like a plan."

"Now, there is something else…"

But he was interrupted. "*Grandpère*, I am older now. Old enough to drive, nearly an adult."

Gilles regarded him, unsure where this was going. "Yes, you are." His heart began to race. He could see tension in the set of Q's shoulders and the way his long brown fingers plucked at the fabric of his jeans.

"I want you to tell me about my father."

Gilles sighed and took a deep breath. "It was a long time ago. This is what I wanted to talk to you about. Perhaps I should have done so many years ago. I thought I could protect you here and that you did not need to know all the details."

"It's important for me to know. If I am to know who I am, I need to know what I come from."

"Q, listen to me. We are happy here. Our life is good. I want you to think about who you have become. You must be proud of who *you* are. You have your whole future ahead of you. And that is more important than the past." He sighed again. "Please sit, and I will tell you."

"*Grandpère*, the past *is* important." Q raised his voice and took hold of the back of a chair at the table. As he pulled it out, it scraped across the tiles.

Gilles sighed. "Sit, then." He took a deep breath. "Your father did a terrible thing. Twelve, thirteen years since. Jean-Michel Antoine, le Comte de Carolet is your father, but…"

"What thing?"

Gilles hesitated and then he knew he could put it off no longer. "He became a traitor to France."

The crease between the boy's eyes deepened. "What are you talking about?"

"He worked for the DGSE in France. This is the Directorate-General for External Security — *Direction Générale de la Sécurité Extérieure*. Now it is a different name. I don't remember it." He shrugged. "Like the MI something over here. The details of its operations and organisation are not made public, but at one point he was detailed to search for a leak." Gilles smiled without mirth. "Ha! He was detailed to search for the traitor, and so was searching for himself." He shrugged.

"I don't understand." Q frowned.

"He worked as a deep cover agent for the Russian KGB, since he was a student. For years he gradually worked his way up in his career, keeping his hands clean."

"What? But that's rubbish. All that happened in the 1950s, during the Cold War, not recently."

"I'm afraid you are wrong, my boy. There is still a big business in spying across Europe, both through the internet and with people in certain positions. Your father infiltrated his way into French government and associated with people who had direct access to important and key roles."

"This is outlandish. It can't be real." Q placed both fists on the table in front of him, and Gilles could see his knuckles whitening.

He carried on, knowing he must finish what he'd started. "He met with naval officers, too, but it was government officials from whom he gained most of his information. He was very charming and tried to lift sources as well as gaining information indirectly. This is true, Q. Apparently, before approaching his targets, he learned about them, their families, their tastes, their weaknesses. He invited them to his house and gave them dinner regularly. He was *le Comte*. They were flattered, I suppose. He fed our people little snippets of information about the Russian military, which he said he had gained in the course of his work. It was either false or useless, I understand. But this is how such people operate. At first he asked for nothing in return, and he gained their trust."

"I don't believe you. It's all too far-fetched."

"No, it is not. There are several cases. Some are very well documented. Your father would give the person he was courting little presents — not too expensive, but if they accepted and appeared to be corruptible, then he knew he had a chance. He was clever. He worked slowly, slowly over several years."

Q rose from his seat and paced about the kitchen with a fierce, dark scowl on his face. "You said he had charm. I've heard it said of me. What must people be thinking? Who knows of this? People will never want me close again. People will not trust me."

"Q, I tell you this because you asked me. You said you were adult enough. This was in the past. People here do not know or do not remember. You are who *you* are, not who your father was. You were correct. It is best that I tell you of these things, especially since Madame Garot and her daughter are visiting here from our village."

Gilles watched with a growing dread as expressions of shock and horror spread across his grandson's face. "That's why you haven't wanted me to go to Slater's Cottage. Ah, *mon Dieu*. The Rosses will learn of this. This old French woman will tell them. Grace will hate me." He turned on his heel and rushed from the room. Gilles heard the front door close with an almighty crash. He leapt to his feet and charged up the hallway, but by the time he opened the door, Q was a long way up the lane.

Gilles returned to the kitchen and as he rested his hands on the edge of the sink, his head sank onto his chest. Then, he scraped his fingers through his hair.

"*This* is why I did not tell the boy," he said to the empty air.

CHAPTER 30

Excusing herself, Angela hurried out into the hallway as the doorbell rang.

It was not Gilles but Q who stood on the step. She was surprised, for Q had been able to come and go from Slater's Cottage for many months now, and usually came in through the rear door with no more than a casual knock and call. He frowned as she opened the door, and his eyes looked dark and haunted.

"Hello, Q. I'm afraid Grace isn't in. She's cycled across to Milly's house to return a book."

"I haven't come to see Grace." He looked pinched and strained. Then, in an unusually harsh tone, he asked, "Have your French visitors arrived?" When she nodded, he went on, "I wish to speak to Madame Garot, please."

He pushed past the astonished Angela and went into the sitting room. Angela followed, announcing, "This is Q Richard, Madame Garot. He is the grandson of…"

The boy stood with a rigid back just inside the doorway and cut across Angela's introduction with a flood of French directed at Felice Garot. The woman dropped her knitting and stared at him, startled. Q's French was too quick for Angela to follow, except for a few phrases. Felice Garot answered with equal volubility.

Suddenly the boy cried out, "*Non! Ce n'est pas vrai!*" He turned to Angela with a look of devastation. "*Grandpère* told me all this. It cannot be true. I can't believe that, but now she says it too."

Madame Garot half rose from her chair and Angela recognised a look of compassion on her face. "*Mon pauvre garçon*," she said quietly. She turned to Angela. "It is true."

Q made a strange, choked sound. Turning, he pushed past Angela only to collide with Grace on the threshold.

"Hi, Q. I've…"

He thrust her aside and rushed out. The slam of the front door reverberated. Grace stood gaping.

"Mum, what on earth's the matter with him? What's happened?"

"Come in, Grace, and sit down. Q's been questioning Madame Garot. About his father, I think." She turned to the French woman. "I'm so sorry. Q must be very upset. He shouldn't have burst in here and spoken to you as he did. He's Captain Richard's grandson. I think you must know Gilles Richard?"

"*Oui*. I know him. Since I was young. Marie was a friend of my mother."

"Yes, of course." Angela shrugged and shook her head as she sighed.

Grace sat on the edge of her chair. "What about Q's father? If Q's upset, I ought to go…"

"No, Grace," Angela interrupted her. "I think it might be best to let Q be on his own for a while. I'm sure he's learned something … something that has distressed him." Turning to Felice Garot, she said, "I think we must ask you to tell us what Q said to you. Tell us about *le m'sieur* his father."

"Yes, I will tell you, but it is a terrible thing. The poor boy. *Il est distrait*. I understand, he learns today only of this terrible things? His *grandpère*, he has just told the boy?"

"Told him what?" Angela said, hearing the hiss of Grace's breath.

"*Capitaine* Richard does not speak of it to you? The poor boy must learn of this today," she repeated but did not continue.

"Learn what?" Angela demanded through her teeth.

"Why, that his father, *le Comte*, is a traitor to his country. To France." Felice's tone was dramatic.

"Traitor?" Angela and Grace said in unison.

"But yes. You did not know? It was in all the newspapers, on the radio and on television in France. Not so, here in England? It is a long time since." She shrugged, and a puff of expletive came from her lips.

"Oh, my Lord," Angela whispered and took Grace's hand as she collapsed onto the arm of the chair in which her child was hunched.

"The agencies seek for him everywhere across France, but poof! He is gone. He escapes. He lives there, Russia or wherever, since that time."

"Poor Q. Poor Gilles."

"Mum, is it true?" Grace sounded piteous.

"I think it must be. I knew Gilles was not telling me something. I never guessed this."

Grace sprang up and whirled from the room. They heard her feet pounding on the stairs and her bedroom door banged shut a moment later.

"*La pauvre petite*. She likes this Q? He is her…"

"Her boyfriend, yes," Angela filled in mechanically. "Felice, this is a dreadful thing you've told us. Awful for Q and his grandfather."

Angela turned one way and then the other, but she knew she must hear it all if she was to help Grace through this.

"Yes. For them it was a tragedy. Everyone stares and talks of it. *Capitaine* Richard did not wish his daughter to marry this one, this Antoine, but he is rich and lives in his chateau near to

St André de la Marche, or in another house in Paris. Gilles Richard is not wealthy also. *Le Comte* says he loves Bettine Richard and will not be refused. She loves him also, and *Capitaine* Richard must give his blessing for the marriage, but he will not."

"So, what happened?"

"Bettine, she runs away with *le Comte*. *Bah!* She is a foolish girl, that one. They go to Paris, where he is working, and they marry anyway. Then she is expecting his child. This one must be Q. Next we all hear that they search for him, and he is disappeared. She is left alone. They question her for many hours. When they let her go, she must return to her home. The carrots are cooked, as we say in France. It cannot be changed."

"So, they came here, to England."

"Well, yes, but then Bettine is very ill. I understand she dies here. Marie Richard says to my mother not to tell where they go, and this we do. But now my mother is dead. And Marie also."

"Yes, she died about five years after Bettine, and Gilles Richard was left to bring up the boy on his own."

"*Le Comte* is a bad man," pronounced Felice Garot, blinking solemnly at Angela. "I hear he needs the money for his expensive life in Paris. But he leaves his young wife and the child."

"Yes. He has done some terrible things, and leaving her alone… He must have been bad, or perhaps desperate."

"So now you know all that is true."

"Gilles knew you were here. I think he must have only just told the truth to Q in case he heard it elsewhere, but we knew nothing of all this. I can only imagine how they are each feeling."

CHAPTER 31

Gilles paced the kitchen, unsure whether to go searching for Q or wait until he returned, which he must do eventually. He could be anywhere, hiding and thinking through all he had heard.

He wondered what he should do or say when the boy returned. This was territory where Marie had been so skilled. He was sure Angela would also be wise about the right way to tackle such issues. He wanted to call her. No, that would not be fair. This was his responsibility. Anyway, she was so mercurial with him. One minute he thought she was coming to him, and the next she distanced herself. It was partly his own fault. He had kept away just before and while these French visitors were here. She had already given so much of her time and energy to him when Q had been in hospital. Now this thing had returned to haunt him. She wouldn't want anything to do with his family.

Should he have told the lad when he was young? He wouldn't have understood all the ramifications as he did now, but perhaps he would have come to understand gradually and more naturally. But he could have worried all these years and wondered what it all meant. Children often got half a story and scared themselves needlessly.

An hour passed before he heard the door again, but the footsteps hammering up the stairs did nothing to calm his jangled nerves. Gilles hurried down the passageway and sped behind his grandson. Without waiting to knock, he pushed the bedroom door wider to see Q stuffing T-shirts and underwear into his school backpack, books and biros strewn across the bed.

Taking a deep breath and trying hard to sound calm, he said, "Son, my boy, what are you doing? You cannot run from this. Please sit and we'll talk some more."

The boy continued with his head down. He flung open a drawer, and grabbing some jeans he wedged them into the bag.

"Please, Q." Gilles stood, helpless. He made to put his arms out to the boy, but Q shoved past him, turning his shoulder away to get through the door. Gilles listened to Q banging around in the bathroom.

When he returned with his toothbrush and a razor, they followed his clothes into the bag. "You should have told me. Everyone must know except me."

"They don't. Believe me, they do not. And even if some people do know, it has nothing to do with who you are and what you have become."

"The Ross family know. That Garot woman will have told them everything by now. I'm not staying here for everyone to be pointing their fingers at me and watching me for every error, waiting for something to go wrong."

"Q, I told you about your father now because you said you were an adult who could handle the information. Listen to yourself. You're not sounding or acting grown-up." Then he lost his cool. "You're sounding like a boy in a temper. Stop these tantrums and listen to me, Q."

The boy glared at him before he thrust past and ran down the stairs.

"Wait. I'm sorry. You're worrying me. Please, let's talk." Gilles stood at the top of the stairs and watched as Q opened the old front door and let himself out. "Come back! Where are you going?"

Then the door banged again and Q was gone.

The last thing Gilles heard was footsteps receding as Q ran down the lane.

Hours passed, and Gilles was more restless than he had ever been. Cruising around in the car had not found the boy. If he'd hitched a lift, he could have gone in any direction. He had tried time after time to contact Q by phoning and texting.

He shouldn't have raised his voice and accused the lad of childish temper tantrums. Q was mixed up and wretched. To learn such an awful truth was bad enough, but believing that all who knew him were ready to blame him for every small mistake because he was his father's son must be unbearable. Q's naturally wild temperament was causing him to be reckless, and Gilles was worried and guilty for handling it all so badly. Normally he aimed for greater calm, and tried to be rational with the boy, but he had seen red at precisely the wrong moment.

Later in the evening Gilles could not resist the desperate urge to see Angela, share his concerns, and receive some sensible advice. He went to Slater's Cottage and rapped on the door. It was Grace who rushed down to open it. From her disappointed expression, he gathered that she must have believed it would be Q, ready to talk over his troubles with her.

"Grace, is Q here with you?" he asked anyway.

"No, he isn't."

"Is your mother in? I must speak with her."

Angela came into the hall. He stood where he was on the step and shrugged helplessly.

"Gilles, come in. You know Felice Garot is here. Is Q all right?"

Before they entered the sitting room, he took her arm gently. "Angelique."

She turned.

"The boy is gone. He's taken his things and his picture of Bettine." His voice sounded odd and harsh.

"Oh, Gilles." She put her arms around him.

Tears came to his eyes. "I'm so sorry. I bring yet more trouble. You will despise me. I tried not to come. But I'm so worried. I need your view. You are always so wise."

"Oh, I'm far from that," she whispered. "Come on in. Maybe he will come back soon, and we shall look back on this as a minor hiccup."

She released him. He took a deep breath and stepped into the room.

"Madame Garot." He nodded. Despite his weariness, he shook her hand politely before he slumped onto the sofa and covered his face with one hand.

Felice Garot excused herself and stood, but before she left she said, "*M'sieur*, your grandson is young and impressionable. No-one blames you or him for what happened, and you have acted honourably. Memories are short. Others do not judge. We do that for ourselves often more harshly than we should, and I see you are your own most fearsome judge. Take heart. All will be well. Give it some time."

He looked up at her with a new and powerful respect.

Grace stood listening, and then after the older woman had left the room, she whispered, "She's quite awesome," before retreating upstairs.

"Grace is finding it hard to process all this, but she's aware that we need to talk." Angela smiled without pleasure.

"It's one thing after another. I'm so sorry," Gilles said. "I handled it all wrong, I think, because I was so anxious."

Angela's arm was warm around him, and he let his head rest on her shoulder. "I'm sorry too," she said. "You have listened to my troubles, put up with me prevaricating and being so unsure of myself that I couldn't come to you. Having to place the children before you. Together, we'll get through this."

He leaned towards her. "May I?" He kissed her lips, gently, tenderly, before pulling away. He tasted the tears that seeped from her eyes and ran down to the side of her mouth. "My love, my peace," he muttered, before wiping her eyes with his thumbs.

CHAPTER 32

As the Garots left for the next stage of their journey and the front door closed, Angela leaned against it with a great sigh. Grace ran upstairs and picked up her phone to send Q a text.

The next morning, birds singing in the ecstasy of the dawn chorus drew Grace from a fitful sleep. She lay listening for a moment, then misery washed through her. Five days! Q had been gone five days and she'd had no word from him.

She still couldn't quite believe that he had left without even saying goodbye or leaving her some message. As if she cared at all about who Q's father had been or what he had done. She thumped her pillow in frustration. It had nothing to do with Q or herself. Surely Q couldn't be thinking she'd mind? Yet why else should he have vanished like this? She could understand something of the shock and deep sense of shame Q must be suffering. It was important to be able to admire and respect parents as well as love them. Q could barely remember his mother, and Jean-Michel Antoine not at all, so he had perhaps built up a picture of his father as someone of whom he could be intensely proud, perhaps some romanticised hero.

Now, thank goodness, the Garots had left. Madame Garot's soulful looks and whispered asides to her mother had been driving her mad. Since Monday she had been waiting for her phone to ring. She had texted again and again. Nothing. She hardly left the house, afraid people would question her, because Debs said the whole village was speculating about Q's abrupt departure. No one seemed to know the real reason. Everyone supposed he'd had a major quarrel with his grandfather. Next week the new term was due to start again, and Grace could scarcely bear the thought of having to go. She knew all the girls would pester to know what was wrong.

In the midst of the birdsong — the piercing sweetness of a blackbird; the whistling thrushes; one blue tit scolding another who must have come too close — she heard a cuckoo. The first one of the spring. She and Q would have recorded it in their wildlife notebook and had fun sparring about who had heard it first. Now, it seemed pointless. She turned her face into her pillow and sobbed.

Her mother called up. "I'm taking Ranger for a walk to the quarry. Do you want to come? It's a lovely day. I'm sure it will do us both some good."

"No thanks."

"Are you sure?"

"I'm sure." She knew she sounded irritable but didn't care.

Sometime later, she heard the clack of the letterbox. She shot out of bed and ventured downstairs. An envelope lay face-down on the mat. In the empty kitchen, she tore it open with shaking hands.

Darling Grace, Q had written,

I thought I'd go abroad right away and let you all forget about me. Seems I'm from untrustworthy stock and even though I wouldn't let you down, I don't think I can take all the talk and finger-pointing, and you don't need that either. After a while you might think any problems are my fault, and I don't want to live with that hanging around.

I don't want to go without seeing you once more, to explain how I feel properly. Maybe you won't want to know, now you must have heard all the gossip about my father. I'll wait at King's Cross Station until four o'clock on Friday. Please don't tell anyone where I am, especially not Grandpère because I know he'd only try and make me come home and I can't face it. That French woman will have spread it all around the village. Come if you can. If not, then you know I'll always love you. I couldn't ring. Someone stole my phone while I was sleeping.

Q.

Friday? That was today. Grace sprang up just as Angela came in through the back door with the panting dog. "Time you got dressed, Grace. It's…" she started to say. Then she saw the letter in Grace's hand. "Is that… ?"

"He's… I can't say. I can't tell you."

"Is it from Q?"

Grace hid the letter behind her.

"Grace, is it Q?"

She hung her head and nodded.

"Thank heaven. Where is he? Is he all right?"

Grace heard the relief in her mother's voice but continued to avoid eye contact. "Mum … I can't tell you. He says I mustn't tell anyone where he is, especially Gilles. And you'd tell him, wouldn't you? Q says…" She choked on her tears. "He's going abroad."

After a moment, Angela said quietly, "I suppose Q doesn't realise quite how selfish he's being."

"Selfish? He's not! He's devastated and upset." She wiped her nose on the back of her hand and sniffed.

"Hasn't he any idea what this is doing to Gilles? Gilles has lost everything; his wife; his daughter; his country, even. Q is all he has. Oh, I know they have a few rows now and then. Herd bulls sparring is all it is, and quite usual at Q's age. Gilles thinks the *world* of the lad." She spread her palms and took a step towards Grace. "If he pushes Q a bit hard sometimes, it's because he's over-anxious for him to do well in life, and now Q's intending to throw everything away."

"He's afraid it may have spread around the village about his father. People will judge him and think he'll be the same." Grace faltered, and great rivers of tears flowed silently down her face. She dashed at them with the back of her hand.

"If anyone ever knew, I'm certain they've forgotten long ago." Angela passed her a clean tissue from her pocket. "Felice Garot and Jeannette have gone. They didn't see anyone to tell. We shan't repeat it. People know Q for who *he* is, now. Q has really worked himself into a state over this, hasn't he?"

"I suppose so." She gave a great gulping hiccup. "Mum, he wants me to go and meet him. You won't stop me! Will you?" Grace sounded agonised and unsure. "I need to try and persuade him to come home."

"Tell me where he is. We don't need to tell Gilles just yet. Perhaps we can meet Q and persuade him to come back."

Grace breathed out. "He's in London. He's waiting at King's Cross this afternoon."

"So, you want me to drive you into Peterborough to catch a train?"

"Oh, Mum, will you?"

"If I don't, you may not get there in time. The bus takes an age." She paused. "Grace, I want to come with you. No, don't say anything." She held up her hand. "I do believe Q needs someone more than just you to talk to him. He needs an older adult's perspective."

"I'd like you to come." Grace wavered. "But … but Q says…"

"Leave Q to me." Angela tried to make her voice brisk. "And don't worry. I won't be hard on him. We better get going, but I need to pop next door to see if Pat will let Ranger out for a pee in a couple of hours, since Debs is at work. Perhaps she'll go to the quarry and leave Ben his food too."

Grace lunged at her mum and gave her a crushing hug, then dashed for the stairs.

A couple of hours later, as the train drew slowly into King's Cross station, Angela glanced across at Grace, who looked pale and tense. She watched with sympathy. How hard it was to be young.

Crowds spewed from the train and onto the platform. Grace dived between people pulling huge suitcases on wheels, men in suits, women with sensible shoes and small cases and a young couple hanging onto each other. Angela tried to keep up, but she wasn't as quick to spot ways of nipping around people. She hadn't even reached the barrier when she saw Q leaning against a pillar, his hands thrust into his pockets, a small black backpack over his shoulder. He wasn't watching all the people rushing past. He was staring at the ground, looking morose and unkempt. He might have been mistaken for a rough sleeper, with the shadow on his chin and his clothes looking grubby and wrinkled.

Grace must have called his name because his head jerked up and she rushed into his arms. They clung together as if standing on the edge of an abyss, his cheek resting on her dark, curly hair. Then Grace was looking up into his face, talking with an earnest expression. Q looked away from her and searched the crowd. Angela hurried forward. On impulse, she reached up and quickly kissed his cheek, aware of the roughness against her lips.

"Q, thank goodness we've found you. We've all been so, so worried."

He flushed a dull red. She had time to notice he looked rather ill and strained before she hastened on. "Don't blame Grace for telling me and letting me come with her. I must talk to you. You can't go away for good. There's no need." She glanced around. "We can't talk here. Let's go over there."

Together they headed towards the coffee shop, with Grace clutching Q's hand.

"You two sit there and I'll sort out food and drinks." Angela waved her hand in the direction of a small metal table. As she headed for the kiosk, she glanced over her shoulder, half afraid that the two young people would dash away together.

As she returned with sandwiches and hot drinks, she watched Grace leaning towards Q with a pleading expression while the boy stared down at the table. Twice he shook his head.

Angela sat opposite and sent up a silent prayer. "You know, Q, no one except Grace, Debs and I know anything about your father. If they ever did know, no one remembers, and they certainly won't learn it from us."

Q darted a quick look at her before lowering his gaze to the tabletop again. Angela signalled for Grace to remain silent.

"Where have you been sleeping? Not rough, I hope."

"I couldn't get a room," he mumbled.

"And you haven't had a lot to eat either, I expect? Have your drink and eat that." She nodded at the sandwiches. "It'll make you feel better." Then she added, "We didn't tell Gilles we were coming here. He's too desperately unhappy about you. I know you two often rub each other up the wrong way, but it isn't *really* important, is it? I'm sure you know how much he cares about you. After all, he hasn't anyone but you, now, especially since your mum and grandma passed. With you gone, he's *utterly* on his own and he's distraught with worry."

The boy swallowed and nodded. "I know. I … I don't want to upset him, but…"

"And Grace," Angela cut in with a deliberate smile, "I can't have you breaking her heart, can I? And you certainly will if you leave us now."

"Mum!" Grace said.

In an obvious attempt to sound adult and in control, Q said, "I … can't decide on the wisest course; on what would be best for everyone."

This time, Angela hid her smile and reached out to touch his forearm. "The wisest course, dear Q, is to come home and prove to us all, but most of all yourself, that you don't intend on throwing away your life as your father did his. Let me tell you something. It wasn't simply greed that made him do what he did. Mainly it was human foolishness. Something of which we're all capable at times. He was in financial trouble with the estate, that's true, but he was desperate to give you and your mother a good life, so he took a stupid risk. A wrong one, yes. Perhaps a criminal one, but he wasn't only thinking of himself. He begged your mother to go with him, but she wouldn't. She knew the life would hold too many uncertainties, and you were only a baby. Instead, she brought you back to Gilles. He and Madame Garot told me all this after you left. He'd have explained it all to you, I'm sure, if you hadn't rushed off."

Angela paused. Grace's gaze was fixed and worried, but Q still had his eyes lowered.

"I know it must have been a terrible shock, Q." Angela tried to steady her voice and quell the tears that threatened to spring up. "It might have been better if your grandfather had told you long ago, and let you grow up with it gradually, but he wanted to save you pain. Q, come home with us. Show Gilles you have strength and are proud of who *you* are now. Look people in the eye and they'll see you are totally trustworthy."

Slowly, the boy's eyes raised to meet hers. "You're sure no one knows about him, my father?"

"Quite sure. Oh, people are gossiping. You know how they are. But everyone thinks you and Gilles quarrelled and you left because of that. We can soon prove them wrong if you come home with us. Simply say you've been on a visit for a few days."

After some moments of silence, Q muttered, "I suppose I have been rather a dick. Sorry."

"Not at all," Angela said, and Grace rubbed her cheek against his shoulder. "Sometimes, when things get really bad, it's so easy to blow matters out of proportion. There's nothing wrong with making a mistake. It's part of learning and growing. The only shame is in refusing to admit when you've been wrong and not trying to put it right. Gilles won't be angry with you. I can guarantee that."

CHAPTER 33

Angela had regretted not seeing Ben for a couple of days, but he had been well looked after by Pat Singleton, who had taken him some food and hot soup in a thermos flask in the usual way, leaving it hidden by the great boulder. She reported that she hadn't seen Ben, but the food had disappeared, and the empty box was returned.

As Ranger scrambled ahead, Angela climbed the stile into the quarry and landed among the flowers. As she approached the hiding spot for the box and flask, Ben shuffled out of the woods.

"Hello," she said cheerily. "I hope you've been all right. I had to go to London, but my friend said she'd make sure you had food."

"Aye, the other missus was good to me," he said. "I went to Peterborough once, but I didn't like it. So, I never been again. London, never. My travels were bad enough."

"I went on what I hope was a mission of mercy, so to speak. I think it will have helped a friend."

"You're a good one, so I think it will," Ben said, looking at her directly for once.

"I wish I could sort out my own life," she said. "Still, I suppose it will all work out eventually, one way or another."

"That's my experience," he said. "It works out. I'm happy enough here. Might not always be easy, but still… You have to go for what's right for you at the time. Can't mind others too much. They'll go their own way and then you'll be left. Time's short. I learned that."

"Do you ever regret anything?" Angela asked on the spur of the moment.

"Oh aye, I do. I should have taken my chance when I had it. I could have had a young lady for my wife and companion, but I was too scared to step up, see. Turned me silly, and her bitter, as I heard. Sorry for that, always. But I have the birds and animals here. Mind you, if them motorbikes keep on, I might not have those either." He looked glum.

"I don't think we'll have to worry about that much longer," Angela told him.

"Oh aye? Shan't be sorry to see the back of that racket."

"Absolutely," she responded. Her mind was still on what Ben had said before. Time was short. Grace would go on to university or somewhere else. She shouldn't let her life pass her by.

"No regretting," Ben said. "Got to go. Things to do."

She watched him shuffle away, his feet still encased in plastic held together with string.

As she walked back home, Angela was deep in thought, her head filled with Ben's words. Life could still be exciting and full of possibilities. She had some catching up to do.

It was while she was preparing dinner that evening that Angela decided to tell the girls something of Ben Cooper's background. She made no mention of Miss Brooks, and the brief part the postmistress had played in his early life. She was retiring shortly anyway, to go and live in a bungalow in one of the new townships on the edge of Peterborough.

Angela described the effect Ben's experiences in the army must have had on his sensitive nature.

"Poor old thing," Grace said. "He must have had such a sad time."

Debs said in a tight voice, "Do you mean to say he's actually Alan's uncle?"

"That's what Pat next door told me."

Their conversation changed course, but soon Debs left the kitchen and a few minutes later, Angela heard the front door.

Debs didn't reappear until dusk. She came straight into the room where Angela was sitting.

"I've just come from talking with Alan. I asked him to join us for a nightcap. I hope that's all right?"

"Of course. You don't have to ask permission. This is your home too."

Debs disappeared upstairs and when she came down again, she was wearing her crimson dress and a pair of hoop earrings.

When he arrived, Debs offered Alan a drink, and they all sat around the hearth, trying to appear relaxed.

At last, Debs spoke. "Alan and I have an idea. We'd like your opinion on it. It concerns Ben."

Angela was surprised. "Ben?"

"It's that old shepherd's place across the back meadow. It's on Moondreams House land, but if old Mr Troughton didn't mind, we thought we might renovate it and Ben could use it. It would be a lot drier and warmer than the derelict railway hut. What do you think, Mum? It's close to the woods. He could come and go as he pleases. If he wants to sleep out in summer, he can, and if he wants to use it in winter, it's there."

Angela thought before she answered. "It's a wonderful plan … if we can get David Troughton to agree, and Ben too. He is such a creature of habit, you know."

"You'd be the one to try and persuade him," Debs said. "He trusts you now. Alan's been increasingly worried about him for quite a while, haven't you, Alan? The old boy is getting on."

The farmer nodded. "He's always rejected help, until now."

"He'd have Ben at the farm to live if he could be coaxed to come, but we know that's too much to expect. He's been offered help in the past, but always refused. You've made this connection now, so…"

"Yes, it would be too much for him to live with someone, now. He'd never cope with that, I'm sure," Angela said.

"If anyone can win his agreement to this plan, it's you." Debs smiled at her mother. "We went to have a look at it earlier, didn't we, Alan?"

"Yes, the roof is reasonably sound. Just a couple of slipped tiles that need pushing back. The beams inside are okay. Floors are all right. Needs new glass in the windows and a decent door." This was one of the longest speeches Angela had ever heard him make.

"You can fix all that." Debs looked up at him from her place on the floor, where she leaned against his chair. "There's a sink already in there, with a cold tap. It needs a good scouring. In fact, the whole place needs a damn good clean. We could do that, Grace, couldn't we?"

"Of course. And I could get some material from the market in town and make curtains, while Q is studying. Something cheap and cheerful."

"I think," said Angela, not wishing to dampen their enthusiasm but needing to be realistic, "that any furnishings had best be kept to the barest minimum."

"Angela is right," Alan said. "Poor guy has been used to sleeping on the hard ground."

"We thought a plain bedstead and a chair. There's a fireplace, too."

"Ben won't light fires. He's afraid of flames," Angela told them.

"At least if Alan hangs a new door, he'll be able to shut out the cold winds and the damp."

"Maybe we could even persuade him to wear some clean clothes," Grace said and pulled a face.

"Let's not go too fast." Angela's tone was dry, but she was sad. "Tell me what happens if Ben simply refuses to make use of the place? I won't force him."

"Of course not, but you will do your best to persuade him to at least go and look at the place, won't you?" Debs pleaded.

"I'll certainly try," Angela assured them. "I think it might be better to wait until the autumn, though. When it begins getting cold again and winter's coming."

"It'll take that long to fix it up. Neither Alan nor I have much spare time," Debs said.

"We can work up there on Sundays, if you agree?" Alan looked down at her and stroked her shoulder.

"When I'm not on weekend duty." Debs nodded and smiled up at him.

"I don't want to throw a dampener on all this, but it really depends on David Troughton. This old place is on his property, strictly speaking. If he disapproves, then we're back to the beginning. Shall I go and see him?"

"That's a plan," Debs said.

CHAPTER 34

Angela was starting a baking session when Grace came rushing into the kitchen. She was out of breath, her hair was sticking to her face and neck, and she puffed out her words. "Quick, Mum. Phone the police. There are two lads beating up Ben in the quarry and Q's fighting them." She half sobbed with fright. "They stopped tormenting Ben and started on Q."

Angela snatched her phone from the worktop and called Jack Marsh as she grabbed the poker from the sitting room. She and Grace tore outside, banging the door shut behind them, and panted along the lane to the quarry.

"There are two of them," Grace gasped. "They had Ben in a corner and were threatening him with sticks. Q just hurled himself at them." She gulped for breath. "Q hit one of them and knocked him down, but the other punched Q's eye. I legged it to you."

"I've no idea what I'll do with this." Angela waved the poker in the air. "Where's the dog?"

"He's with Q. I hope so, anyway. What if he's hurt too, or he's run off?"

"Well, he hasn't followed you home, so let's hope he fended these thugs off."

To their relief, there was no sign of the two lads when they burst into the quarry. Q sat propped on a stone, mopping at his face with a bloody corner of his T-shirt, and Ranger lay at his side, panting.

Ben hovered around, hopping from foot to foot and wringing his hands. "Oh my! Oh my! What will we do?"

"Ben, are you hurt?" Angela asked as she knelt by Q's side. "Let me look at your face. You're going to have a really juicy eye. Here, use these tissues. They're clean. Probably better than your T-shirt, anyway."

"I'm all right," Ben said. "Oh dear. That lad came just in the nick. But they started hitting him instead. Oh, dear me…"

Jack Marsh arrived, looking red-faced and unfit. "Don't often have to run like that. Just as well I was at home in the office. What happened then, lad?"

Grace knelt next to Q as he told his tale. "Ranger started barking, and one of them ran off and got on his motorbike." He dabbed at his bleeding nose. "I managed to catch the number of one of the bikes."

"Young thugs," grunted the policeman. "Don't worry, Mrs Ross. We'll get them, and they'll be up in court. It'll be actual bodily harm rather than grievous, more's the pity." He turned to Ben. "You okay, mate?"

"I got things to do," he said, casting around with his eyes, as if looking for an excuse to go. "I'm all right, thanks."

"Q stopped them." Grace turned to Q, who had staggered to his feet, and linked her arm through his. "You were amazing," she said.

"We'd better get you home and get an ice pack on that eye," Angela said.

"I wouldn't hang about here, Ben, if I were you, although I don't suppose those louts will come back." Jack Marsh patted him on the shoulder. "I'll message the Peterborough Force. Should find those young devils without too much trouble, since Q had the gumption to get a number. Wish everyone had as much sense."

"I'm afraid it's not going to enhance your looks in the short term, Q," Angela said as they walked him back across the fields to the village.

"There's always something, isn't there? I'm always in some trouble," Q said.

"Not of your own making this time. We're proud of you for this," Angela said.

Soon after, Angela went to see David Troughton about renovating the old shepherd's hut. As she approached the house, Annie appeared and was heading towards the front door, too.

"Hello," she said. "Are you going to the teashop?"

"I wasn't. I've not been yet. I need a word with Mr Troughton."

"Ah! He's not back from town yet."

"Perhaps I'd better come back."

"Tell you what — it's about time we got to know each other better. Would you join me for a cup of tea, and perhaps a slice of one of Natalie's famous cakes?"

"That sounds like a wonderful idea."

They went in through the front door and turned left.

"This is the old dining room. Natalie has also converted a similar room at the back for young mums and their children."

"It's beautiful in here." Angela gazed at the Georgian décor.

"Wait until you see what Natalie has baked. She's a genius." Annie led the way to the counter, where she introduced the young woman waiting to serve them. "Hi, Nats. This is Angela. She's been in the village for a while now, and is waiting to see David. Can we have tea and cake, please?"

After they were seated, and Natalie had delivered their order, Annie asked, "So, how are you finding things here? I heard that you met Ben in the quarry."

"News travels fast," Angela said.

"Don't mind the villagers on that score. We are like a family underneath it all."

"Pat, next door, said much the same," Angela said. "Yes, I took pity when the weather was so awful in the winter."

"We each have our stories. It's the way of things, but here at Moondreams House we are a close-knit group now. We've been so concerned for Gilles with all the worries about Q's injuries. It seems to have turned out well. That lad is turning into a great young man. I know he's very friendly with your daughter."

"They do get on really well, and now they're campaigning against the motorbike scrambling idea, so that's keeping them busy."

"We're all pleased to hear it, I must say. Good for them."

"We've been very concerned for poor old Ben. He's so frightened by the whole thing. Actually, that's the reason I've come to see Mr Troughton. Can I share our idea with you? I'm so nervous about speaking to him."

"He's fine, these days, but he used to scare me witless." Annie leaned in closer and lowered her voice. "Back in the day, when I first came here, he was such a recluse and I had to ask him if I could rent the ballroom. Well … that's history. It's all worked out and here we are. So, whatever it is, I know he'll listen."

Angela shared the plan that Alan and Debs had come up with for the conversion of the little hut for Ben, and Annie was very encouraging.

"Hey, perfect timing." She nodded towards the sound of a car on the drive. "We've more or less finished here. Let's be quick and catch him. I'll introduce you."

"That would be marvellous. Thank you so much."

They turned the corner as David got out of his car and was crossing the courtyard. The introductions were made before Annie left, waving her crossed fingers at Angela. David led the way through the kitchen and along a dark corridor before they re-entered the large hall. Instead of heading to the dining room where Tea and Sweet Dreams was, they turned in the opposite direction and went through a door to one side of an enormous marble fireplace. It proved to be a study that smelled of oak panelling, old books, and ash. There was an enormous old desk and two tapestry chairs on either side of the fireplace. David indicated that Angela should sit, and he took the seat opposite. Despite being old, the chair was surprisingly comfortable. Angela sat back, trying to look relaxed.

"Right, Mrs Ross. How may I help you?"

Angela explained about Ben as best she could.

"Oh yes, I know of old Ben. He has quite a history."

"I've been concerned that people might think I'm being a busybody, arriving here and taking on responsibility for feeding him," Angela said.

"Don't look so worried, my dear Mrs Ross. Anyone who can give that stubborn old soul some help is a good person, and well done to you."

Angela smiled with relief before she launched into her proposal. "It wouldn't cost you anything at all." She spoke earnestly. "My daughter and Alan Cooper will provide what's needed and do all the work between them."

"I'll tell you what," David said, "we'll do a deal. If they will do the work, I'll pay for the materials, such as the new door and the glass."

"Really? That's marvellous." Angela couldn't believe it.

"Mmm. The property is mine, so I should do that much."

Angela heard a tiny hint of the formidable man he used to be, but then he smiled and his whole demeanour changed, and she relaxed again. "Mr Troughton, I can't thank you enough."

He stuck out his hand and she took it. He was a funny, old-fashioned man in his suit and tie, but he had a kindly heart, it seemed.

As she sat with her daughters that evening, Angela had decided to take the opportunity to tell them about her decision regarding a deeper relationship with Gilles, if he'd still have her. Ben's words had replayed in her head for long enough. Debs seemed to be about to take another step away from home, and Grace would surely come around to the idea. Still, she hesitated, and her unease hung between them.

"Mum, can we discuss something?" Grace blurted unexpectedly.

"Of course." Angela took a deep breath and waited, wondering what on earth was coming next. Grace glanced across at Debs, who shrugged and then nodded.

"You know I said I didn't want you to live with Gilles."

"Mmm."

"Well, I've decided I was being a bit immature and selfish," Grace said. "Q thinks it's a good idea, too."

Angela found she was struggling to suppress tears of relief and happiness.

"We're both genuinely pleased. It's what Dad would have wanted," Debs said, and looked away in her awkwardness.

"Thank you, both of you. Thank you so much." Angela held out her arms, and Grace rushed across to give her a hug.

Then she pulled away and looked at her mother with an impudent grin. "Q says he'll never get used to calling you *Grandmère*, though."

"If Gilles still wants me," Angela said. "It's been a long and difficult time. So much has happened, and it's taken me quite a while to be ready to move on. I've worried about both of you, too."

"What do you mean, worried?" Debs asked.

"You lost your father. Gilles will never replace him, I know that, and so does he. It's important that you always feel you can talk about him, even if Gilles and I are together."

Despite her relief, that night Angela lay awake until the early hours of the morning. When she finally fell asleep, she had a weird dream about a ladder she could not climb because she was frightened of falling. On waking, she decided to go and see Gilles as soon as Grace and Debs were gone for the day.

No more would she put off important conversations. She'd done that with Ade, and it was her biggest regret.

CHAPTER 35

As he stood at the window, Gilles tried to raise the enthusiasm for work. The day was fair, and Q was back on track and seemed to be working hard. But today Gilles felt listless; he should have been eager to be out in the fresh air, but he wasn't.

Then, his stomach gave a flip as he saw Angela coming down the lane towards his house. The wind caught her dark hair and she brushed it from her face as she approached. Her hips swayed, and her cotton skirt blew. As she neared, she looked at him and he raised his hand in greeting.

"Angelique," was all he could manage through the lump in his throat as he held the door wide for her to enter. His heart thumped. "Please…" He ushered her into the living room. Her faint perfume was heady as he indicated a chair for her to sit on. He sat opposite and waited.

"Gilles, I…" She shifted in her seat.

"*Mon coeur*," he said softly.

This seemed to give her the courage she needed, for at last she spoke with greater confidence. "Oh, Gilles. I've spoken with Grace and Debs. Grace must have spoken with Q. I've been a fool. Ben said… Oh, never mind that now." Her shoulders relaxed, and she leaned forwards. "I want to be yours. I…"

Gilles flung himself onto his knees in front of her, taking both her hands in his. "You don't want to wait?" he asked, his head on one side. "Are you sure?"

"I don't want to wait. Yes, I'm sure. I'm so sorry. I've been a fool and messed you about."

He stood, raising her to her feet, and drew into his arms. "Are you really sure?"

"I've never been more so."

"My love, my dearest." He kissed her gently, hesitating. Her lips were soft and warm and yielding beneath his own. His hands cradled the back of her head and then one arm came around her shoulders, holding her close. He was aware of her curves and knew his need for her was strong. She must feel him. His desire was potent. She arched against him.

"I want you. This minute," she whispered. "I can't wait any longer."

"If you're sure. I would like to go outside, kick off our shoes and walk on the soft, cool grass. But for now..." He took her hand and led her up the stairs.

At the weekend, they decided to hold a celebration. Gilles, Q and Alan came to Slater's Cottage.

Angela was greatly relieved that both her daughters still seemed genuinely pleased about her impending remarriage. "Gilles is a kind man," Debs said as they worked companionably in the kitchen. "He'll take care of you."

"And I him."

The three of them talked of little else but future plans. Angela said she would insist on a quiet wedding. Gilles had said he was happy to leave the choice to her. Debs surprised her mother when she stated that she'd like to continue living at Slater's after Grace and Angela moved to Gatekeeper's Cottage.

"Well, for a little while, anyway," she added. "Maybe I'll buy out your share, or if I get an offer of somewhere else we could rent it out."

"So, for the time being, I'll have two homes." Grace did a twirl with the dishcloth.

Helped by Gilles and with the money from the sale of his motorbike, Q was well on the way to affording a small, second-hand car. He and Grace spent hours poring over adverts in the local papers and online.

In August, when Q got his A-level results and found he had two As and a B, Gilles gave him the rest of the money he needed. He accepted his place at Sheffield to do an engineering degree. "It's just over an hour away," he told Grace. "I'll be home quite often."

Alan and Debs had worked hard on the little shepherd's hut, so all the structural improvements were complete by the end of July. Q and Grace whitewashed the walls and scrubbed the floors, and Debs scoured the sink and polished the brass tap until it shone.

"Now it's all ready for Mum to do her stuff," Debs said as she closed the door for the last time.

Angela had thought a lot about how best to approach Ben on the subject of his new home. She was determined to respect his choice, even if it seemed unreasonable. He would be living much nearer to the village if he went there, but she was sure people would not disrupt his privacy. No one else in Waterthorpe knew the true reason for the work being done on the hut.

It was early October before Angela broached the matter with Ben. Now that she and Grace had moved to Gatekeeper's Cottage, she usually drove up to the quarry for her daily visit.

It was beautiful, dressed in the russet and gold of autumn and burnished by the low sun, which appeared suddenly now and again. She saw a couple of deer grazing in a shaft of light. The woods were silent and empty, another world. A slight frost had whitened the grass when she saw Ben waiting for her near the entrance. He was bent and gnarled like the trees among which he lived. He was swinging his arms and clapping his hands for warmth. She noticed that the gloves she had knitted for him the previous December now had holes. She would have to make him another pair before the cold weather arrived.

"A bit nippy this morning, Ben. You'll be glad of your hot tea."

"I will that, missus. I have to admit," he said, gazing at her with a mournful expression, "that I'm not looking forward to winter's cold coming along."

Angela saw her chance and took it. "It must get pretty chilly down in that old railway cutting."

"My word, it does sometimes. But mustn't grumble. I can manage." He gave her a wry little smile. "Have to, I guess."

She took the plunge. "Well, actually, I've a suggestion to make about that. Do you know that old shepherd's hut over on the other side of the woods?"

"Used to use that at lambing time," he said unexpectedly.

"It's been done up a bit. New door, glass in the windows. The man at the big house who owns it says you'd be welcome to sleep there, if you'd like?"

The was a pause.

"It would be a lot warmer and drier than where you're living now," Angela continued in a casual tone. "And it's really close to the woods."

"Well now," said Ben slowly. "I dunno."

"No one would bother you there, like when those lads had a go. And the twiggy couldn't get in. You could come and go as you please."

"Hm, I s'pose I could."

A chink of sun pierced through, and blue sky appeared through the patches of grey.

"Much nearer, too, for me to bring you meals." Angela had resorted to cunning. "Not that I mind coming up here," she added. "I have to exercise Ranger, but I could just walk him around the meadow there."

There was another pause.

Then, Ben said, "I might go and take a look."

"Why not? No hurry to make up your mind."

"Maybe I'll take a walk around that way later on."

"Good idea," said Angela, smiling. "The door will be unlocked, so you can pop your head in and see what you think. Well, come on, Ranger. We'd better get our walk done. It looks as if it might rain. See you tomorrow, Ben."

He was waiting for her again the next morning, out in the open. She thought he had a nervous air, and her heart sank. Probably he wouldn't entertain the idea of going to sleep in the hut, and all Alan's and Debs's time on it would have been wasted.

Almost at once, Ben spoke. "Took a look at that shepherd's hut yesterday. My word, it has been smartened up."

"What did you think?"

"Bit too posh for me." Ben looked at her from under his brows and his tongue passed over his lips.

Anxiety bloomed in her chest. "Oh, surely not, Ben. Only a bed and one chair in there, isn't there? Did you sit on it?"

"Well, just for a moment I did."

Angela thought she detected an air of suppressed eagerness. "You'd be able to sit in comfort to do your 'digitaries', and maybe write some poems when you felt like it."

"The man at the big house said it'd be all right?"

"He certainly did. He'd like you to use it. It's not needed for anything else just now." She hesitated and then decided to go the whole way. "Actually, Ben, the man who put on the new door and mended the windows is your nephew, Alan. Your brother Joe's boy. He'd be really happy if you used it. I think he's going to marry my elder daughter, Debs, next year, you know."

For a dreadful moment Angela thought she had overplayed her hand. He stood gazing at her with a look of mild shock.

"Well, fancy," Ben said. "My nephew Alan. I did hear Joe had a boy. And he says I can live in that smart place? My word. It's amazing, truly amazing."

CHAPTER 36

On several Sundays, the quarry resounded with the growl of engines, the blare of a tannoy, and motorcycles roaring up and down the village street to the pub. Club members were careful to be polite to local residents, but some of their young supporters, riding out from the city, got involved in quarrels with local youths. Twice Jack Marsh had to be called to settle drunken disputes.

Grace and Q's petition appealing against extending the use of the quarry as a motorcycle scrambling centre became the forerunner of a torrent of phone calls and letters protesting to the county authorities. A special meeting was held to discuss the matter again, and this time, the vote against the project was unanimous.

It proved a busy season for them all. Gilles and Angela arranged their wedding for late autumn, when the gardening season was quieter and there was less to do. Gilles could leave some of the jobs at Moondreams House to others while they took a week's honeymoon in the West Country.

Angela's dress fitted her perfectly, with a fuller skirt falling from her hips. The lines were accentuated by copper-coloured piping down the front seams, contrasting with the creamy fabric. The long sleeves each ended in a point, which rested on the backs of her long-fingered hands. Tiny cream flowers encircled her hair. She carried a simple bouquet of dried flowers and wheat with tiny blackberries and rosehips hidden among the delicate blooms. Gilles turned to watch as she came to him and was overcome with love for her.

"I am so lucky," he whispered.

She smiled up at him, looking radiant. "I love you," she mouthed.

That evening, when all was done, and peace had descended, Gilles and Angela changed out of their wedding attire and wandered hand in hand down to the lake. They stood looking down into the water.

Angela's thoughts turned briefly to Ben. "I'm very relieved Ben has a dry place to sleep when he wants. I know he still sleeps in the forest, but later, when there are frosty nights…"

Gilles took Angela's hands in his own. "*Mon coeur*, Angelique," he whispered into her hair. "I love you so much. Your compassion, your good sense … your passion when we are alone." He chuckled.

Angela smiled and turned her eyes to the night sky. He followed her gaze. "Just look at that," she said, marvelling at the stars. "Makes all our troubles seem small, doesn't it?"

"Our past troubles," he reminded her, and puller her closer.

"You're right." And in a moment of clarity, she added, "I've never been so happy."

They looked at each other then, full of hope for their future. Gilles took her hand and gently led her towards the willow tree, where branches caressed the water. He pushed aside the falling fronds and led her into the secluded den within. Kicking off their shoes, they let the damp grass caress their toes.

A NOTE TO THE READER

Dear Reader,

I've set this story in and around Moondreams House and I hope you have enjoyed meeting again some of the characters from the first two books in the series as well as meeting new ones.

Ben is based on an old recluse who lived in a disused quarry in Northamptonshire. He lived in dire circumstances as a rural rough sleeper. His name was Tom. Gradually, my mother grew to know him and took to feeding him in the way described in the book. He did his 'digitaries' and wrote her little poems after hearing that she, too, was a writer. Nobody knew what circumstances had affected his retreat from society but his sweet nature and gentle demeanour ensured that, when he passed away, the village clubbed together to provide him with a decent funeral. I couldn't resist including him in this story, although I have invented his background. All other events surrounding this character are also from my imagination.

My thanks again go to the people at Sapere Books for their cover design, editing, and marketing expertise. They are all skilful and I'm so grateful to have the backing of this publishing team. Without them, I as a writer, and you as a reader, would miss much.

If you enjoyed reading *Finding Happiness*, perhaps you might leave a brief review on **Amazon** or **Goodreads**. It doesn't need to be long; a couple of sentences will more than suffice. It will inform readers when choosing a book and would be a huge boost to this author. Thank you.

If you would like to know more about my writing, my website is **www.rosrendleauthor.co.uk**. Here you can also **sign up for my newsletter** where I often offer free gifts and timely access and information about forthcoming books. I'd love to hear from you, my dear reader, and you are able to chat with me via **Facebook** or **Twitter.**

Thank you, again, and I hope we will meet soon through the pages of one of my other books.

Ros Rendle

Sapere Books is an exciting new publisher of brilliant fiction and popular history.

To find out more about our latest releases and our monthly bargain books visit our website: **saperebooks.com**